The Half Mother

A Novel

Shahnaz Bashir

hachette INDIA

First published in 2014 by Hachette India
(Registered name: Hachette Book Publishing India Pvt. Ltd)
An Hachette UK company
www.hachetteindia.com

1

ISBN 978-93-5009-788-5

Hachette Book Publishing India Pvt. Ltd
4th/5th Floors, Corporate Centre,
Sector 44, Gurgaon 122003, India

Typeset in Adobe Garamond Pro 11/14
by InoSoft Systems, Noida

Printed and bound in India by Bhavish Print Solutions Pvt. Ltd., Chennai

THE HALF MOTHER

Shahnaz Bashir was born and brought up in Kashmir. His essay, 'A Crackdown in Natipora', was anthologized in *Of Occupation and Resistance – Writings from Kashmir* (Tranquebar 2013). He was honoured with the university gold medal and the Shameem Ahmad Shameem Memorial *Kashmir Times* Award in 2007.

Shahnaz teaches creative journalism, and narrative and literary reportage at the Central University of Kashmir, where he is coordinator of the post-graduate media studies' programme.

The Half Mother is his first book.

Praise for *The Half Mother*

'A debutante author goes beyond the headlines for the other side of the Kashmir story.' – *Forbes*

'Widely lauded in literary circles for its bold new voice.' – *New Asian Writing*

'Finding the truth in fiction.' – *Hindustan Times*

'Well-written and engaging.' – *Times of India*

'Bashir draws a picture of idyll with tenderness… His language is…at its best when it evokes the terrain.' – *Indian Express*

'The novel has those unique strengths so missing in our fiction today... *The Half Mother* brings to light one of the greatest human tragedies of the covert war in Kashmir.' – *The Hindu*

'Realistic dose of fiction.' – *Asian Age*

'…lyrical descriptions and minute details of settings and places point at [the author's] ability to conjure images of that place and time.' – *Business Standard*

'A mother's nightmarish quest for her missing son.' – Firstpost.com

'…*The Half Mother* adds a nuanced layer to the local narrative, caught in the uncertainty of life and death.' – *Hard News*

'*The Half Mother* goes beyond headlines and misinformation to bring you an insider's view of Kashmir.' – *Bangalore Mirror*

'The prose does take you into the heart of Kashmir…' – *Millennium Post*

'Shahnaz Bashir's novel is based on Kashmir and its struggle. But what's unique is a woman fighting for her right.' – *Statesman*

'…he [Bashir] attempts to tell the untold story of Kashmir.' – *Sakal Times*

'*The Half Mother* is certainly in a different league from the other works of fiction born out of the Kashmir conflict so far. The book impels the reader, at once, to admire the grandeur of graphic artistic expression and relive some of the forgettable memories.' – *Greater Kashmir*

'Shahnaz has created a niche for himself in the list of the emerging conflict writers of the world… His prose is nothing short of lyrical.' – *Kashmir Life*

'*The Half Mother* marks the daring debut of Shahnaz Bashir, another rising star in the literary firmament of Kashmir…lavishly elegant and delicately beautiful.' – *Criterion*

'It becomes almost impossible for the reader to read through the narrative without gasping for breath and without trying hard to hold back the tears.' – *Rising Kashmir*

'The love of a mother for her disappeared son finds such an expression in *The Half Mother*, that all else loses significance.' – Contributoria.com

'A moving novel.' – *Kashmir Monitor*

'...these stories need to be told – they are screaming to be told. To leave them untold would be such a loss for humanity. Also, it's said that one thing more difficult than the beginning of a novel is knowing how to end it. The challenges would require deft handling of the content and mastering the craft of storytelling. Shahnaz Bashir's debut novel *The Half Mother* does all these and more.' – *Reviews*

'The book is graphically written, with a passion that transports the reader into the emotional world of a mother searching for her son.' – *Citizen*

'We are introduced to a brittle Haleema, wishing for death. Bashir describes her home poetically – filled with loneliness and heartache. A must read!' – Writerati.com

For
Mutee Ahmad, who was born alongside this book

And for
the mothers and sons of Kashmir

دریا، کہسار، چاند، تارے   کیا جانیں فراق و ناصبوری

Darya, Kohsaar, Chaand, Taaray
Kya Jaanay Firaaq-o-Naasaboori

Rivers, hills, the moon and stars
What would they know of separation's indelible scars!

Judaai (Separation), Baal-e-Jibreel
– Sir Allama Muhammad Iqbal

Book I

1

A reverie in retrospect

Snow, dust, roads, paper planes, plastic bags, pictures, papers, smiles, auto-rickshaws, guns, doors, voices, faces, mirrors, dolphins, textures, flags, burnt wounds, walls, shadows, silences, cigarette stubs, scraps, songs and pigeons – bits and pieces of memories randomly refracted through her reverie.

'The greatest sufferings bring the greatest hopes, the greatest miseries greatest patience, and the greatest uncertainties lead to the greatest quests…' She mumbled the Imam's words on waking up. She woke up hating herself, remembering the pleasure of the dreamless sleep she had before dinner. She hated having to believe she existed, to feel she was conscious. She hated the smell that sleep brought. She wished she were dead.

As night invaded the house, Haleema sat on the broad ledge of her kitchen window and looked out into the moonlit darkness. She hated the moon now.

After Imran had been taken away, she had fallen to the ground and helplessly looked up at the sky. Her hair had fallen loose about her face, as if it had been pulled in a fight. She had continued staring at the inky sky, searching for God and howling with helplessness, but she could only find the moon in it – the moon: cold, still and silent, and indifferent in the halo of its own glow. Haleema hated the moon since then – it was a reminder of her loss, nothing else.

Now, as she sat on the ledge, she unfolded her fatigued legs – limbs made brittle by excessive walking – steadily, as if preventing her knees from cracking. She stretched them flat, reclining against the cold wall. As usual, Natipora was dark; there was a power cut. She had grown accustomed to its erratic appearance. And to candle-lit nights. A pear-shaped hundred-watt bulb hung from a wooden rafter on the ceiling. The leaf-like flame of a candle swayed and did a gentle dance in the silent darkness. The candle sat above a clay oven in the corner, the wax profusely weeping down its sides already.

'Dear collard greens, apologies, for you shall be cooked without salt once again,' she told the vegetable, which she had cooked for dinner. She loved collards, and even more so when served with hot rice. She loved to look at them once cooked well with an extra dash of oil. And she cooked them often. The vegetable reminded her of meals with Ab Jaan and Imran. Of happier times. Times full of conversation and laughter.

'Where have you disappeared? Where do I look for you now?' she now called out to the often-misplaced wooden ladle. 'Here you are! Where have you been? I have been looking for you everywhere,' she said, finding it hiding behind the clutter of steel tureens. She put the ladle back in its right place, in the space between two stacks of bowls.

As the night passed, the darkness continued to grow thicker and slowly anaesthetized everything in its path. Haleema continued to brood, listening to the termites gnawing away at her kitchen door. She ignored this now-familiar sound and instead felt her cracked heels with her calloused fingertips.

After washing down half a dozen pills with a glassful of water, she tore open an orange to subdue the metallic aftertaste of the pills. She carefully stacked the torn pieces of the rind, topping the stack with the pith and the slippery bitter seeds, and threw them into the bin. Then once again, she was back on the ledge, now studying the frayed edges of her dupatta that badly needed washing. Her eyes did not leave her wooden gate.

The absurdity of her loneliness was difficult to express in words. Her head was filled with flashing visions and buzzing memories. She slipped into a reverie, a surreal reverie, almost like a voice, and not yet a vision – something little more than the slightly vague dream she'd had after meeting Abdus Salaam, the barber.

Haleema's gaze hung dreamily. She murmured absentmindedly, just as she would have rehearsed the wedding *madrigals* for Imran:

The colour of everything is sorrow,
the colour of the moon is sorrow,
the colour of the streets is sorrow, and
the colour of memories is sorrow.
The colour of my heart, in its own heart, is sorrow.
The colour of my breath is sorrow,
the colour of sorrow is sorrow.

A cat pounced on its prey in the attic, and the noise it made startled Haleema. She strained her ears. A long silence followed. Her eyes once again settled on the night, outside the window and on the wooden gate. Ab Jaan's rusty Hercules bicycle, with its deflated tyres, still stood upright against the tin shed.

2

Life in the plum orchard

In his life, Ab Jaan dabbled at various odd jobs. He worked as a cart-puller but the job didn't fetch much of a living. He tried gardening and proved to be a mediocre gardener. He was fired as caretaker of an English doctor's farmhouse after there was a theft in his absence. He failed as a construction labourer when stonework began to hurt his back. His paltry salary as salesman at a Punjabi cloth merchant's shop in Srinagar too was unsatisfactory. And then, just after he married Boba, he became a candy maker in Sohan Lal's factory. Desperate to spend more time with his new bride, he could not wait for the factory bell to toll. He would hang his gold-plated watch on a nail dug into the wall beside the furnace when he came for work and would periodically glance at it to ensure that he left much before the factory bell pealed thrice to signal the end of the day. He would then impatiently scurry down the roads and alleyways of Natipora, half-shaking hands with the people he knew along the way. Or he would greet them improperly, barely acknowledging their pleasantries. Such haste, such love.

Ab Jaan would bring Boba fish-shaped and star-shaped candies wrapped in tinted cellophane, and sometimes ring-shaped candies that she would slip on her ring finger. He would make them from the vestigial remains of the confection at the factory.

But when the factory's furnace began to frazzle his hands, Boba solemnly noted it and insisted that Ab Jaan find another job.

Ab Jaan roved about Srinagar until Abdul Gani, his childhood friend, informed him of a tailor's position at a factory which manufactured leather goods. The factory was owned by Philip Russell, one of the many Stetson-wearing British businessmen in Kashmir. It was in Raj Bagh, across the Jehlum. Russell always rode to it on horseback, the horse's gallop bouncing his stiff head up and down, with half his legs covered in well-polished, shiny black stiefels.

Ab Jaan needed to scrawl an application for the job in whatever little English he had picked up from his father, who'd died when Ab Jaan was in the third grade at the government-run Urdu school. So one bright sunny morning, he stuttered all the way to Raj Bagh, crossing the Jehlum in a boat, to submit his application. Across the river, he took a shortcut through a cherry orchard and marvelled at the parrot-bitten fruit and the cherry-scented air filled with the music of diverse birdsong. He tendered a crudely drafted letter, stating how desperately he needed the job, any job:

> Janaab Philip Saheb
> Lord Sir,
>
> I poor, request you merciful self with the beg that I needs a job. We poor self will gave you kind self hundred of thanks. We poor self will got very happy if you gave job. We poor self to remember you so much for any job to the end of us life.
>
> I want your good self forgive the mistakes if any on my darkhaast letter to you good self. I beg for one time extra.
>
> Thankyou. Thankyou. Thankyou.
>
> Your humble servant
> Ghulam Rasool Joo

Ab Jaan's real name was Ghulam Rasool Joo, but no one called him by his first name. At work, he was mostly known as Rasul Joo, and in Natipora he was famous as Ab Jaan.

He could not get the tailor's job; instead, he was apprenticed to a master tailor at the factory. He felt proud of himself for getting the job and the unexpected acceptance of his rough application.

When Britain entered the Second World War, the demand for pelt and pelage-lined leather jackets (with their seams tasselled), goat-hide trench coats, furred gloves and moccasins soared. The vanguard English army sought safety from the stinging chill of the ubiquitous snow on the frontlines. Philip Russell in Kashmir exploited the opportunity; he doubled his production and ordered his factory employees to work overtime.

Ab Jaan now brought home gashes on his fingertips, causing Boba to cry over them, her tears licking his fingers like viscid glycerine. He began to think of changing jobs once again, when he found an advertisement published in a corner of the front page of an Urdu newspaper:

Office of the Project Officer
Central Public Works Department
Haft Chinar, Srinagar

REQUIRED

Applications are invited for the post of Cook (one post only) from those candidates who know cooking and can demonstrate it. A test in this regard shall be conducted in the office of the undersigned at Haft Chinar, Srinagar, on the 15th of this month, 9 a.m. sharp.

Qualifications: No bar.

Age: 37 years max.

The applications should reach the said office within seven days from the publication of this notice.

Sd/-
Project Officer

Ab Jaan considered it and thought of giving it a try, even though he didn't know how to cook. Boba helped him remember the names of all the Kashmiri spices and condiments. He crammed the Urdu terms, mugged up the crockery.

'What do we put into rogan josh?' Boba would ask incuriously.

'Cumin, cinnamon, clove, cardamom, fennel and...fennel and...' Ab Jaan would reply, forgetting and recollecting, sucking in air through his teeth, rolling his eyes.

'And pinches of finely chopped coriander, for the smell,' Boba would add with a smile.

In front of a selection committee at the CPWD office, Ab Jaan confidently demonstrated his cooking skills. He was appointed as cook among four other candidates. Soon, along with his cooking skills, Ab Jaan began impressing the officers with his ideas on architecture and drafting. In a few years he was promoted to junior planning assistant, and with the hike in his salary, he bought a black Hercules cycle.

Ab Jaan's cycle became a wonder in Natipora. It outran all the other bikes in the neighbourhood and was the only one with a headlight and a steel basket under its handlebar. He loved it like one loves a pet. He washed it every Sunday and pumped air into its wheels – a little less in the front wheel than the rear one – carefully. To prevent them from rusting, he cleaned the spokes with a rag soaked in kerosene. He greased the cycle's crankset and its cassette and checked the bottle-shaped steel dynamo clamped on the rear wheel. Finally, he would check the screws of the brakes and the pedals before this weekly ritual would be over.

Soon Boba gave birth to a beautiful girl. Ab Jaan named her Haleema, and she became the apple of her parents' eyes. When she grew up, Ab Jaan got a small red child's seat fixed on top of the cycle frame for her. He would take her for long rides every evening, while narrating endless stories from Kashmiri folktales: *Gulrez* and *Gulistaan–Bostaan*. She frequently interrupted him with questions about Prince Ajab Malik or Princess Noushlab or the beautiful garden where the two would meet.

Haleema was eight when tuberculosis killed Boba. Having deeply loved her and his daughter, Ab Jaan promised himself he would not marry again. He toiled to continue Haleema's education but failed when the household gradually began to fall to pieces. One day, Haleema went to her school and donated her textbooks and notebooks to her classmates, snotty girls with loose, rough, greasy and carelessly plaited hair, all uniformed in sky-blue shalwaar-kameez. Tearful, Haleema's teachers and friends embraced her for the last time. Her class teacher wrote on her black, bottle-rubbed glossy *mashq*, the wooden slate, in Urdu:

Hamaari Pyari Haleema, Hum Dua Kartein Hain Ki Tumhari Zindagi Bahut Khoobsurat Ho.
(Our beloved Haleema, we wish you a very beautiful life.)

Under it, her classmates affectionately followed suit in longhand, with culm-daubed Multani-mud ink repetitions, making the *mashq* look like a workbook page.

Haleema devoted herself fully to household chores then: she milked the cows, winnowed the rice, washed, cleaned, mopped, swept the leaf-strewn compound with a besom and pounded on red chillies in a large stone mortar with a wooden pestle taller than her. Slowly, the chores became a habit; the habit seeped into her and then became a part of her being.

The closest neighbour of the Joos was a woman called Shafiqa. After Boba's death, Shafiqa informally assumed the role of Haleema's mother. She would frequently visit the house in the mornings and evenings and voluntarily educate her about chores till Haleema learnt almost everything. Shafiqa helped her cook fish with drumsticks, collards, radishes.

Natipora was three kilometres away from Lal Chowk, the centre of Srinagar, to the south. The locality grew sparser and finally transformed into vegetable farms, paddy fields, bush lands, poplar grooves, and plum orchards. The Joos lived on the edge of one. Here the hum of the neighbourhood changed from the hubbub of urbanity into a trill of birds and insects. A dirt road led further into the fields towards the east. It was this road that separated the commune from the scattered encampment of houses to the south. The main road lay perpendicular to the dirt road.

The house in which the Joos lived was an old, seemingly crumbling three-storey building with traditional Kashmiri lattice windows. The front windows were filled with multi-coloured stained panes. Its walls were made of sun-baked bricks and rough aspen wood which had never seen the carpenter's plane, and were unevenly mud-plastered on the inside. The earthen shingles of the roof had weathered with time. The white paint on the termite-ridden windows had begun to flake, and the dowels had started to come loose off their mortises. Their attic stocked hay and gunnysacks full of fodder. Stray cats leapt, rolled, somersaulted, snarled and groaned whiningly in the attic. And kept breeding.

The Joo's backyard was fenced with Russian poplars, horse-chestnut and acacia trees. Spikes of sunlight winked through their branches. Mossy wooden palisades, pointed on the top, filled the gaps between the trees. Over the palisades, creepers and marrows curled. Their house sat on the edge of a plum orchard – making it seem like a vast farmhouse. In a distant grassy corner, where the earth sloped slightly, two cows, a mother and a heifer, lay tethered to two willow stakes on muddy ground in the shed. Sometimes, when Haleema would bring out the cows, the crows perched on their backs would peck at their skin-deep fleas.

Beside the cowshed was a large chicken coop, partly enclosed and partly cloistered in wire. Crestfallen roosters clucked and gambolled like goons after the hens, running about here and there. One of the hens had a featherless neck. She didn't lay as many eggs as the others did. The roosters found the hen repulsive and rarely copulated with her.

At the CPWD, Ab Jaan retired as senior planning assistant and opened a *waan*, a general provision store, in Natipora. Due to his honesty, people began preferring his shop to the other stores in the neighbourhood. Every lurking, loafing or loitering child rolling a disused tyre radial down the lane would get a bubblegum or candy for free. The curd he sold was considered the best in all of Natipora. His unique, cheap coconut biscuits were much in demand. During idle hours at the shop, he would read the entire Urdu newspaper he subscribed to, even all the advertisements. He would read the columns on the editorial pages along with cup after cup of *nuun chai* twice. He would then cut out the most important news to collect them; a dusty, yellow pile of clippings sat on the top shelf behind his seat.

In his youth, he had been a radical *sher*, an ardent supporter of Sheikh Abdullah. Ab Jaan had even gone to jail once, for six months. But then, one evening, after listening to Abdullah's speech on the radio – in which the *Sher-e-Kashmir* expressed a willingness to support the accession with India – Ab Jaan was disappointed. In a bout of anger, he threw out the larger-than-life portrait of Abdullah of his bedroom.

Ab Jaan enjoyed invoking the memory of his last job, the way the project men drilled and blasted through the heart of the Upper Munda summit at Pir Panjal, burrowing into the mountain with giant iron claws. He vividly remembered how those rusty German machines worked their way into the tunnel – a tunnel that cut a three-hour journey to less than ten minutes. He marvelled at the risks involved in the workings of the dynamite, the inclement weather that flirted with their plans, and the way he and his colleagues had, after all, triumphed and muscled through the mountain.

'I still remember those deafening explosions. The business of blasting is horrible,' he would often tell some of his elderly customers.

Since Haleema was Ab Jaan's only child, rules dictated that the person she married ought to be a *gari-peth* to the Joos – the husband had to live in his wife's home rather than in his own home.

Haleema married a medical assistant from a Srinagar nursing home, who began having an affair with a nurse at the hospital within two months of the wedding. Haleema learned of the affair after finding two roughly folded pink tickets from Naaz Theatre in a pocket of one of his pants. As days passed, the doubt intensified. She began rummaging through his clothes for more signs, finding kohl stains and strands of blond hair around the sleeves and collars of his shirts.

Haleema became reticent, and let him go. The marriage ended in a whimper when Haleema divorced her husband in just three months.

She kept only one souvenir from the marriage: a picture that now lay face down on the topmost shelf of a lacquered heirloom armoire in her room. Originally in black and white, the photograph was later developed into a technicolour copy and encased in a glass frame. Ab Jaan had sent the negative to an old office friend who lived in Delhi. The friend had posted it back to him along with the enlarged coloured version.

The photo was taken on the seventh day of Haleema's wedding. The couple had shyly posed for the camera outside the house, in the small lawn that Haleema herself tended, with a disarrayed stack of bricks in the background. The noon sun lit the lower halves of the couple's faces, while shade from a plum tree fell on the other half. A falling leaf was magically suspended in the air above them.

Haleema looked happy in it. Her oval face made her look like Boba. She had worn a maroon bridal shalwar-kameez and sparkling maroon sandals. A pattern of almonds-on-vine goldwork motif ran endlessly along the hem of her kameez and the seams of its cuffs and neck. She had wrapped a matching maroon shawl, heavily embroidered with tinsel work, about herself. A thick plated necklace, crafted with designs out of medieval Indian temples, and long matching earrings adorned her. She held a matching maroon purse with shiny plastic spangles stuck all over it in her right hand, while she held her husband coyly with her left.

The medical assistant looked handsome in his white kurta-pyjama. The kurta's rhinestone buttons went down its neck along a strip of needlework. The hippy haircut made his head look (two-dimensionally) somewhat like a garden spade. He wore coffee-brown leather slippers; a heavy golden watch – part of his dowry – hung loose from his wrist and drooped over his left hand. He stood in an uneasy posture as if he meant to tell the photographer: Hurry up!

After years of her divorce, silverfish now lived and reproduced between the photograph and the cardboard frame. Generations of spiders had woven a grid of gossamer strings around it. Silverfish had devoured its edges and bitten into the leaves of the plum tree that shaded the couple, and even engulfed a branch and some of the bricks. But the insects had spared the two of them.

And it so happened that one autumn afternoon, just some months after the marriage was over, that Haleema developed a retching sensation. The local pharmacist tried to repress it with anti-emetic medicines, but she began to get cramps. Then a physician advised her to get a gynaecological check-up.

Haleema didn't tell Ab Jaan and boarded a bus to Lal Ded Hospital, the only maternity hospital in Srinagar, by herself. She strode down the long sad corridor of the hospital, seeking a female doctor. It stank of disinfectant. She overheard passing nurses gossiping about expecting women. She sat on a long steel bench and waited for her turn. Some baffled and weary men stood resting their behinds against the wall beside their pregnant wives. They looked as if they did not know what had happened to their wives and what they were doing there.

The doctor had a harsh temperament to her voice. She scolded Haleema as she did all her patients.

'Lie flat on the gurney, face up,' she scolded.

Haleema obeyed.

'Turn on your right side,' she scolded.

Haleema obeyed.

'Turn on your left side,' she scolded.

Haleema obeyed.

She pressed a cold stethoscope onto Haleema's warm stomach.

'You are pregnant,' she shocked Haleema, looking away from her to the window of her cabin and back to Haleema's face.

'You need care,' she scolded.

'Come down,' she scolded.

'Take these medicines and get these investigations done,' she scolded.

Haleema gave birth to a baby boy on the last day of July – a scorching hot day. He was born in a room where raw green tomatoes were wrapped in straw inside a wooden crate to ripen.

His infant babble made Haleema smile weakly. He flailed his limbs about and rubbed his tender chubby hands together. The gentle wisps of his hair felt supple against his scalp. Haleema loved to open his tiny wrinkled fists and clean his finger webs, the lines on his palms and his knotted bellybutton. She would sprinkle Jasmine talcum powder on his neck, groin and armpits, test his feeder on her wrist for the temperature. And sometimes, for reasons unknown to her as well, paint his tiny fingernails red.

He did not resemble Haleema, though – the medical assistant came through in his face. He had the same long face, yet sharper and unflinching eyes. But he had Haleema's dimples and his fingers were short and stubby like hers, with cuticles overlapping the white crescents under the nails.

Ignoring the stark similarities between him and his father, Haleema passionately and desperately lied to herself. She dismissed the similitude and likened the boy to herself, declaring that he was a part of her being. 'See, my dimples, my fingernails,' she would readily offer while praising the baby before people could begin saying that he resembled his father.

Ab Jaan named the boy Imran. He replaced the worn baby seat on his bicycle with a new blue one. He brought him toys and dolls even before Imran could regard their value, like a made-in-Taiwan dinky bus with a rotating umbrella on its roof. Imran would respond to the moving umbrella by fluttering his lips. Ab Jaan also got him a box full of plastic nuts, bolts and strips with a set of plastic tools: a spanner and a screwdriver. The tools fixed the nuts, bolts and strips variously into helicopters, towers and houses.

An airplane that thrummed and flickered angry red lights from under its propellers when its tyres scraped the floor.

A doll that closed its eyes when laid on its back and opened them when straight, with long nylon eyelashes long enough to almost sweep her cheeks.

Then a Tobo tricycle.

Perfumed multi-coloured pencils.

With thick ballpoint pens, Ab Jaan would draw watches on Imran's flabby wrists. The watches with their traces of time would eventually fade away and disappear.

When the boy began to speak, it was clear that he could remember events that had occurred before his birth. He remembered the Imam's reception on returning from the Haj. The boy could even describe the Imam's clothes: the grey summer *pheran,* a loose tweed gown, and an immaculate white turban. He could tell the colour of the triangular buntings, the silver paper trimmings, the festoons of multi-coloured balloons and serrated paper ribbons hanging in the

Haji Imam's courtyard: red, green, orange, white and blue – all tied to a jute string. He knew who all had gathered at the Imam's house, including his own mother Haleema.

He could also strangely recall a bridal procession travelling in a jeep along the banks of the Jehlum at Solina – where the river separated the suburbia of Srinagar from the urban – and the brass band, the bandmaster, the bagpipes and the beating of drums that followed the jeep. And, surprisingly, the skidding of the jeep and its fall into the river.

In late autumn the hens hatched their eggs inside the barn. Haleema would show Imran the cheeping chicks. The mother hens looked angry and chuffed from motherhood. They raised their quills and pecked at the hands that touched their children. But they were helpless against the eagles that dived and stole their chicks.

Not far from the house were their ricefields, where hovering dragonflies mated while flying, the air thick with the buzz of their wings. When the rice would ripen in early autumn, Ab Jaan would amuse young Imran by making scarecrows out of his old clothes.

Imran's childhood had as many injuries as the other children: he broke his bones jumping from high walls and tree branches; gashed his arms running through bushes; scraped his knees while learning how to cycle on Ab Jaan's much-bigger bicycle. The wounds eventually twisted into scars of different shapes, a perpetual reminder of his childhood.

At one end of the orchard was Ab Jaan's vegetable patch. Like all other vegetable patches in Natipora, it was fenced with barbed wire, nailed into willow boles along the edges of the land. The farm had a deep well – lined with moss and ferns – whose water smelt of the earth. The well was partially covered with a platform of corrugated tin, padded with thick grassy cakes of soil. Ab Jaan would stand on the lip of the platform and winch the water out of the well. The water would sluice into a long furrow that branched into the beds of the collard greens, cauliflower and green chilli and *knol khol* and marrow, and bitter gourd and purple brinjal and mint and spinach and green pea and shallot and garlic. The water seeped in the fertile soft earth and brought up insects, rotting leaves and bits of twigs. The flotsam enticed thrushes, goldfinches, mynas, sparrows, topknots, cuckoos and nightingales, who would scurry around to discover a treat of aphids, ladybirds, earwigs, crickets, beetles and grasshoppers.

The birds that darted about the farm always brought back a painful memory for Imran. He had once let his catapult loose on a sparrow that had made her nest in a small hole on a wall. He had killed the bird to impress himself with his sharpshooting skills, which he had not believed he had until the pebble hit the bird right on its rump. He dug a tiny grave for her behind the cowshed, and after completing all funeral rites, he discovered naked chirping nestlings. He tried to redeem himself by feeding the chicks and guarding them from eagles and crows. But one by one all three of them died. To assuage his guilt, he would allow birds to bite into the collard saplings or the bottle-gourds whenever Ab Jaan wasn't looking.

Ab Jaan would hang his wristwatch on the fence in front of him and periodically glance at it to ensure that Imran was on time for school.

After passing the annual school exams each year, Imran would desperately wait for his new set of textbooks. He loved the smell of fresh paper. They came arranged, tied neatly with jute strings hitched on the top. He would knife through the triangular extra corners to separate the fused pages. On the mornings when the results would be announced, Ab Jaan would make it a point to secretly tuck in the new set in Imran's drawer. Once discovered, Imran would gleefully bring out an old calendar to cover the books, the blank sides face out. He would paste stickers on them and then fill in the particulars in the funniest of ways:

Name:	Not important (What's in a name? That which we call a rose/By any other name would smell as sweet – William Shakespeare)
Roll No:	786
Subject:	Kashmir
Grade:	Success doesn't matter, what matters is hard work
Address:	Citizen of the whole earth

He would bookmark the pages with rose petals and peacock feathers. Myths went around in his school that putting sugar on the feathers would one day yield a peacock out of the book.

Another myth: keeping pencil shavings in water overnight made an eraser of it. That folly allowed the stationery stores outside the school to foster – it was they who had encouraged the myth.

There were Red, Pink, Yellow and Green Houses at his school. Each House had to perform scouts' duties on two days of the week. Imran would wear a green ribbon-badge on the pocket of his white uniform shirt that read: I ♡ KASHMIR.

Imran's classroom was on the third floor of a building whose windows overlooked the whole of Natipora: the Joo ancestral graveyard, the shrine of the mystic Syed Taj-ud-Din Wali, the big chinar, the market and the long winding road. The classroom's ceiling was topped with an enclosed mezzanine; Imran and some of his classmates had hidden a carrom board there, and they would sneak up and play during free classes.

Aziz's small narrow shop, which was just outside the school, was where all the children swarmed before and after school. It was a fusty, rundown shop and did not even have a counter – just a few shelves. Aziz would sit on the floor next to his wares laid out on mats of burlap sacks. Big tin canisters showcased a variety of inexpensive candies, biscuits and snacks. Imran was fond of the shop's special, yet cheap, stick candies, cigarette candies and tamarind candies, which would last till he reached the morning assembly.

It was at Aziz's shop that they would chat about the teachers, the syllabus, homework and carrom. They would bet on the brand of sunglasses and shoes Haseena Dar would wear while addressing the morning assembly that day. Mrs Dar had no interest in teaching, but because she was a senior teacher she had been entrusted with the responsibility of imparting physical education to the students.

Imran was good at carrom. Always after the bright red queen, the centre of attention on the board, he tussled to win it first. He had a knack for sending down two to three carrom pucks together into the netted pockets. He released the striker with a restrained shot so that it pushed the other pucks away and remained teetering on the edge of the pocket. He was an expert at the art of rebound too, and would lightly tease his friends after his wins. After getting the queen, he would take pride with a fake arrogance mingled with a light smile. 'Ha ha ha! I won! Again!' he would comically announce in Urdu.

Until 1987, the mezzanine in Imran's classroom was famous only for the secret carrom games. But that year, it became a hideout for local political fugitives. In the wake of 1987's failed elections, the two rival political parties violently clashed against each other. A war broke out between their supporters. One of the parties' supporters from Natipora clandestinely used the mezzanine to hide for months. One day the school authorities called the police and got the place raided. The men were arrested and the door of the mezzanine was nailed shut.

3

Snow

In the long, powerless, dark December nights, Imran would bring his English Reader textbook to Ab Jaan and ask him to narrate stories from it. They would sit by a kerosene lantern in the kitchen. In the pall of the smoke-blackened chimney, the lantern would cast a sick shade on things and faces, and in its sad glow the Joo family would look like three pale ghosts.

Haleema would calmly sit behind her *yinder*, the spinning wheel, on the chowki near the clay oven and spin wool. With a faint smile, she would occasionally glance over her steel-rimmed glasses at Imran and Ab Jaan, both absorbed in a story.

Ab Jaan would lean closer to the lamp, struggle to read the words and interpret the stories, fumbling and sputtering as he went along.

The stories intrigued Imran. He would try to resolve how Kasim could make a bet with Ali for ten marbles over an incredible 'magic' pencil that Kasim claimed could write all the colours: red, blue, green, yellow, black and even white. (It soon dawned on Imran that Ali was stupid enough to not realize any pen could do that: 'write' all the colours!)

Or who would save the innocent Red Riding Hood from the big bad wolf?

Or whether Robin Hood was right in robbing from the rich to give to the poor?

Or marvel about the king who would humbly tour the countryside to learn what people thought of him. He toured to know his faults and therefore to consider them. To consider them and therefore correct them. When the king's people said that their great king had no faults, it made the king sad. For, he was counting on his faults to save himself from the complacency of being self-righteous. To be self-righteous was to begin to be barbaric. That, in an unknown, unconscious way, the complacency of being 'absolutely good' affected his struggle to be himself. Not being yourself, the king thought, ceases your freedom. And risks your optimism. Smokes your dreams. Ends your imagination.

Besides stories, Imran had some strange hobbies too. Habits, rather.

He would mischievously put the *tsalan*, the stoker, amid the live embers of Ab Jaan's *kaanger* while warming his hands over it. He would then slobber his spit on the hot *tsalan*. The hiss of the sizzling spit and the stench would make Ab Jaan and Haleema strain their ears and flare their nostrils. Then they would scold him.

Bored, Imran would dig his hand into his *pheran*'s pocket and reassure himself with his collection of the most absurd things: a slippery horse chestnut, a key fob suspended on a Vicks inhaler, a dysfunctional cigarette lighter, a fragment of a magnet, a pinion of an old timepiece that worked as a spinning top, five green marbles, a pair of flint stones, a dial of an old wristwatch and a hexagonal aluminium twenty-paisa coin.

Once Ab Jaan was exhausted to tell more stories, Imran would pull his *pheran* tautly over his knees and bury his head into the dark tent and rub the flint stones together in its darkness.

In her poorly lit corner, Haleema would strive to keep the stretching thread from snapping as it formed between the tip of the spindle and the fleece. The mild drone of her *yinder* was the only sound that filled the warm kitchen air.

One stinging, frigid January night, Ab Jaan did not ring the bicycle bell as he usually did when he returned home from the *waan*. He almost threw his bicycle against a poplar. He entered the house with a rolled-up Urdu newspaper tucked under his arm, his mood pensive. Haleema understood something was wrong. She adjusted the wick of the lantern, which had begun to smoke, and nimbly ran over to the stove to urgently stew *kahwa* for him. She watched him furtively, his strange silence, his creased brow, and the sullen, serious eyes. He did not smile as he usually would, not even slightly.

'The war has begun,' Ab Jaan said with tired eyes, quietly, almost to himself. *Valley Times*, the newspaper he carried under his arm, had a report about a gun battle in Srinagar: two masked men had shot a police constable at point-blank range and run away on their scooter. The long tussle between the political rivals had finally culminated into war. Young boys had begun sneaking into Pakistan to fetch arms and rebel against the government.

That night, Ab Jaan pulled out his shoebox-sized, partly wooden, partly plastic Panasonic transistor. The transistor had to be slapped or slightly banged on its rickety sides to make it work. Fits of cough would follow and then a long clearing of its throat before it spewed out the news. He tuned the little black dial and adjusted the needle on the wave scale to BBC Urdu. The transistor gave out violent and funny sounds, changing from a hissing station to another twittering, then to whistles, squawks and then unfinished sentences in an unknown language.

Finally the broad, masculine voice of a broadcaster in chaste Urdu confirmed the news in detail. The voice alternately faded and returned. Another station would interrupt the BBC's frequency with an opera singer and Ab Jaan would lean closer and work on the dial to restore the news.

Ab Jaan told Haleema that the frequency interruptions were an attempt by the government to censor the BBC.

One day while on his way to school, Imran saw several men in khaki fatigues at the local Sufi shrine shovelling sand into white nylon bags; some of them were stacking the stuffed bags one over the other. When they fell short of sand, the troops dug out mud from the fringes of a nearby graveyard to fill in the sacks.

Baffled schoolchildren stopped and watched the men do their strange exercise – no one had ever seen bunkers inside the valley. A loop of rifle-wielding men in army apparel guarded their colleagues. The door to the shrine was hardly visible now, with the bunker nearly blocking it. The troops roofed the bunker with long sheets of corrugated tin and placed large stones on it to weigh it down against occasional winds. They then swathed the shelter in nylon camouflage net, hung two navy-blue buckets at either side of the bunker's entrance, and painted Aum in white on each.

The army shooed the puzzled children away.

Ab Jaan was moody that night and smoked two packets of Cavender filter cigarettes back to back. Imran wouldn't dare ask for a story, and quietly watched his grandfather successively puffing the cigarettes to the butt. When Ab Jaan was lost in his thoughts, the cigarette ran up to the stub, burned the filter and made him cough. He quickly stamped it dead in the glass ashtray beside him and lit another. When all the cigarettes were gone, Ab Jaan turned to his old discarded *jajeer*, the hookah gurgling with each long drag.

That *chila-i-kalaan*, the first month of the winter, began with a powdery snowfall, followed by a brief spell of sleet, and then it all turned into a blizzard. *Why have these men come to die in the cold?* Imran thought to himself. He snuggled under his *kaanger*-warmed quilt, listening to the thud of the snow as it slid off the roof and hit the ground near the window of his room.

It thrilled him, as always, to get up early on the day of the *nowsheen*, the first snow of the winter. Snow meant early or emergency vacations; no more frozen feet in classrooms. It meant icicles – suspended like tapering carrots from the slanting edges of roofs – had to be crushed and concocted with sugar and milk into mouth-numbing ice creams. It meant the cowls of snow had to be shaped into caricatures and snowmen, the chill numbing his hands. It meant rummaging the attic for charcoal to be pressed into the faces of his snowmen. It meant pilfering potatoes and eggs from the storeroom, roasting them in the *kaanger* and eating them hot, burning your mouth.

And late in the winter morning…*nowsheen* meant to savour saffroned hot *kahwa* from earless China cups, poured out from a *samovar*, wisps of steam dancing out its spout. *Nowsheen* meant arranging the *hamaams* and the *bukharis*, the enclosed tin braziers.

The birds would dart about on the bare branches of poplars and plum trees and peck at the snow to find any remaining crumbs and grains, which the endless blanket of white would conceal. The cars couldn't be moved from where they were parked. Buses wouldn't ply unless the snow melted to slush.

It also meant twenty hours of power cuts every day.

Inside Imran's cosy bed, with his child-sized *kaanger*, it smelt of heat. As he closed his eyes he fell into a deep chasm of darkness, where absurd, abstract and grotesque shapes appeared and quickly fused, deformed or transformed into something else. And then into something else. The shapes and images kept morphing into larger and larger forms, then zooming out…now small, now large again. Imran slept, the soft sound of falling snowflakes soothing his dream-filled sleep.

That morning he woke up to the sound of a hard knock on his bedroom door.

'Imu, get up, *gaasha*! Ab Jaan is going out to clear the walkway and tap the snow off the power line. Help him, come,' Haleema hollered.

Imran batted his sleep-glued eyelids, reluctant to get out of the warm quilt. He rubbed his eyes and pressed over one with his forefinger. Holding it that way he saw two of everything around him. He threw the quilt aside and jumped off the bed. He put on his woollen bobble cap and the muffler and mittens that Haleema had knitted for him. He parted the cashmilon curtains of his window and drew his forefinger on a steamed windowpane tracing his name on it. *Imran*. He looked out of the window through his name and found the world outside dressed in brilliant white. Only then did he pull thrice at the door of his room to pry it open, jammed as it was from the moisture and warmth.

Ab Jaan had already cleared half the snow from the path that extended from the gate to the entrance, panting every now and then. 'Give it to me now, Ab Jaan,' Imran said, his vapourized breath coming out like smoke. He looked up at the top of the poplars, squeezing his eyes to shield them against snowflakes. The specks looked grey in the air. For a while he gazed at them with reverence, as if someone had rent open the pillow of God.

Half the wooden gate lay buried under the snow. Imran picked up shovelfuls and cleared the walkway. The gate opened with a caustic squeak.

As Ab Jaan and Imran went to clear the path outside the gate, they saw two troops in long khaki trench coats walking towards them. The alabaster-like fresh snow crunched and crackled under their white ball-toed military boots. One of them, a rifle slinging from his shoulder and a crooked forefinger on the trigger, told Ab Jaan brusquely, 'Give us your shovel.'

Ab Jaan thrust the shovel in the direction of the other trooper. The men walked off with the shovel.

Outside, there were dozens of these men, all dressed in olive-green overalls with rifles or shovels, digging a few metres away from the plum orchard. Some of them were filling sand and soil in big nylon sacks, building a bunker near the house. The bunker was constructed at an angle that allowed its small window a straight view of the Joo house.

Confused and shivering with both rage and fear, Ab Jaan thundered at them, 'The bunker will be a nuisance – you will always be intruding into our homes. Our women cannot come out of their houses. Please take the bunker a little away from here.' The trooper with the rifle turned and pushed him back with the butt of his rifle. Ab Jaan fell on the snow and his black karakul hat tilted over his eyes. Imran ran over and helped him stand up.

'We are already tired and here you are… Go away or…' the gunslinger groaned at Imran.

Imran furiously sprinted towards the trooper who had punched Ab Jaan, ramming into his legs and pummelling his thigh. 'How dare you touch my Ab Jaan? How dare…I'll kill you,' Imran screamed and growled fiercely. The trooper tried to push him away but Imran stuck to his leg like an insect. Ab Jaan tried pulling him off the trooper's leg.

Imran asked for the shovel back.

By now a horde of people from the neighbourhood had gathered. Haleema cried and pleaded helplessly with the army. People argued and protested. They rescued Imran from the wrangle. The Imam arrived too. He stroked his straggly beard anxiously and tried to reason with the men. He tactfully managed to stop them from building the bunker inside the neighbourhood. The troopers moved away, and the rest of the people who had gathered to watch the fracas too dispersed.

Imran stood frozen, dazed, gazing with rage at everything around him. Everything – the gate; the path, now cleared of the snow; the shovel, now returned by the trooper; his mittens; Ab Jaan's *karakuli*; the poplars; the falling snow – seemed to applaud him for what he had done. Barefooted, Haleema ran, crying, with a steel tumbler of water towards Imran.

That evening the Joo family sat quiet for a long time, as if in mourning. No one spoke for hours, not knowing what to talk about.

Ab Jaan planted a cigarette on his lips and pondered. The slender stick dangled unlit for a long time.

Imran sat glumly in a corner of his gloomy room, recalling the incident over and over. The memory of Ab Jaan lying in the snow with his *karakuli* tilted over his eyes brought tears to his eyes. Everything in his room looked distorted, yet clearer through the tears.

4

Executive Bond

Before getting the first shave of his life, Imran seriously considered his face in the mirror. *Should I go for it or not*? He had a fair face – with a long masculine nose, sculpted lips and large sharp eyes – now with fine hairs on it, but the stubble stood out under the thick, bridged brows. His classmates had been teasing him about the dense fuzz, so he ran Ab Jaan's razor down his dimpled cheeks, his chin and his upper lip. He thought he looked girlish now. He hid his face under several folds of his muffler even on sunny days, and for several days he blushed when noticed by a smiling Haleema and a chuckling Ab Jaan.

Imran had grown into a tall teenager, and his voice had changed to a guttural one too. In a strange way, he seemed more of a husband than son to Haleema. When he would come into the kitchen and blindfold her eyes with his hands, she would say, 'You are a fool, Imran *saeba*. Try some other trick.'

Then, when he would take his hands off her eyes and pick up a slice of turnip or *knol khol*, Imran would reply, 'There is no other trick.'

'There couldn't be,' Haleema would respond, not looking up from her chore, 'there exists no trick in the world for a son to deceive his mother.'

Whenever he stood beside her, Haleema would consider his height and look up to speak to him. She would feel as if she spoke to someone older than her. Someone firmer, stronger than her. He seemed like her protector now.

On Sundays, Imran would help Haleema in cleaning the puffs of fleece, separating the wool from the thick, distinct, unwanted hair. Ever since her youth, Haleema had spun wool and flogged it to the local shawl merchants of Natipora. She saved the money for Imran's education.

Imran collected his pocket money, coins of one or two rupees, in a *bigwaer,* an earthen piggy bank, that he shook every night to reassure himself. He would poke a knife through the dark slit and pick out some coins to feel them tangibly, and then insert them back again.

He became quite adept at mechanical affairs. In addition to mending household equipment, he made table lamps and electric torches from plastic handles of brooms. When Haleema's *yinder* broke down and started squealing from excessive spinning, Imran mended it. He fiddled with electrical appliances in the house and learned to repair them. He repaired irons and heating coils of heaters and water boilers. It was he who triumphantly discovered the source of the mysterious leakage in the Imam's bathroom at the mosque, where everyone else had failed.

Imran assisted Haleema with the chores too. Sometimes he washed all the clothes, and ironed and scented them with *ittar*; sewed patches onto cotton-leaking holes in pillows, cushions, mattresses and quilts; stitched up the toes and heels of Ab Jaan's and Haleema's winter socks and mended zippers by rubbing candle wax onto them.

All this expertise came from Haleema. She too was a famous name in the neighbourhood. Sick women often sought her advice. They believed in her remedies more than the quacks, especially since Shafiqa was relieved of her stomach ache after Haleema ground some dry herbs for her. Haleema diagnosed enigmatic diseases by holding the patient's feverish wrists. She could point out symptoms and syndromes. Reasons and cures. Apprehensions and hopes. She preferred herbal treatments and insisted on prevention. 'Warm the paste and spread it like jam over a loaf on a collard. Put it right on the carbuncle. You will be fine,' she once assured another woman who had a boil on her stomach.

But all this was before Haleema lost her own health.

Her complaints of breathlessness swiftly burgeoned into a horrible state of suffocation. Her condition began to frighten Imran and Ab Jaan. When she inhaled, she sounded like a drone, and she exhaled like a hoarse whistle.

A physician identified it as bronchitis. He advised her to be wary of dust, pollen, scent and smoke. Below Rx, on the prescription sheet that he tore off his letter pad, the doctor jotted down medicines in an illegible scrawl.

When Imran and Ab Jaan helped a staggering Haleema out of the doctor's clinic, she slouched and rasped hard, huffing, gasping and panting rhythmically. Her cough was relentless and she tottered to sit down after every ten paces. The Dal waters bore a dull sheen beside them. A clouded sun shone on its wind-rippled surface. Haleema leaned against a scraped lamppost while Ab Jaan looked out for a rickshaw. Imran stared at her with bland eyes. He felt like hugging her and crying but he felt shy to do so. Vaguely. It baffled him to see his mother's health deteriorating. It threw up new challenges for him.

Imran maturely assumed all household responsibilities. He began waking up early at dawn and fetch hot *lavasas* from the local baker in the usual crewel bag, which was always hooked onto a nail behind the kitchen door. Ab Jaan would roll a ten rupee note and place it inside the bag. Imran even began to assist Haleema in cooking the meals. Before leaving for school in the morning he would serve her *nuun chai* in a bowl-like cup, soak crumbs of crustless soft bread into the tea and sink a teaspoon into it. She had to be fed the tea in spoonfuls.

Imran would then toss detergent into a bucket of water and immerse Haleema's phlegm-stained handkerchiefs in it. He would wash them in the evening once he returned from school and put them on her *kaanger* to dry. He would sweep the house and mop the dusty floors; wash the dishes and prepare everyone's *kaanger* in the mornings, seeding the fire with bits of discarded egg-trays.

Before he left for school, he would keep Haleema's medicine, her aluminium spittoon and a jug of boiled water with a tumbler by her cot and then deliver a flask of hot tea to Ab Jaan at the *waan*. Just a few years ago, he had been a child and needed Haleema's help to get dressed for school. Just a few years ago, she would brush his hair with her fingers while he involuntarily listened to Kailash Mehra sing on the late morning radio show. And now, it had all come a full circle, him paying back the debt of a son. He had come to relate to the lyrics of Mehra's songs, which he had never understood before, or even tried to. He had grown up too soon.

He grew laconic and wouldn't laugh at the jokes his classmates made during class anymore. He no longer participated in their pranks. He had no desires or complaints. Now, whenever Imran returned from school, he would first note Haleema's pulse and then ask her to give her day's report. He would then replenish her jug with freshly boiled water and empty her spittoon, now overflowing with phlegm. And then he would direct her over her medicines. 'This small white pill after dinner. This peach-coloured one at bedtime. Inhaler, as the doctor said, "SOS"...' He would demonstrate the dosage, tapping on the silver-foiled strips of tablets, trying to match the names of the tablets with the illegible prescription. The only thing legible on the prescription pad was the watermark that read, 'Executive Bond'.

Ab Jaan began taking over more responsibilities too. He took care of the cattle, dropped fodder in their troughs, milked the cows in the mornings and scattered the feed for the chicken. He stopped smoking inside the house. The *jajeer* now lay dusty, disused and cobwebbed, beside Haleema's *yinder*, in a dark corner under the wooden stairs.

5

Tempest

The year 1990. As the insurgency in the valley intensified, the government resigned, paving the way for governor's rule. Tears, blood, death and war followed, as did curfews, crackdowns, raids, encounters, killings, bunkers, an exodus of people, burning markets, schools and buildings.

Shafiqa's sons, Shaheen Bhat – known as Natipora's Einstein for his exceptional talents in science and math – and Imran Bhat – an invincible footballer sobriqueted as Maradona – were the first two boys from Natipora to cross the border to Pakistan.

Then Shabeer Ahmad, the blacksmith's son, was the first in Natipora to fall to army bullets. Twenty-three rounds were pumped into his chest when he refused to throw a Pakistani flag off a telegraph pole.

Then Shafiqa's daughter Rukhsana became the first woman from the neighbourhood to be beaten, in her own compound. Her parents were tied with ropes and made to see their daughter being stripped by a trooper.

And then farmer Ramzaan Dar's ripe paddy was set on fire when he refused to hand over his son Riyaz to the army.

The smell of burning tyres hung in the air of Srinagar.

Hundreds of thousands began to march on every street and road in an endless stream of processions. Men, women, children, old, young – all. Their green headbands, the banners they brandished, the flags they waved, the placards they held, the slogans they shouted and painted on the walls repeated the same word over and over: *Azaadi*.

Once the summer was over, the yellowing leaves began to set up an autumnal aura in the neighbourhood of Natipora. Fern drooping along the brims of wells withered. Cascading brooks in the orchards fell arid. The gush of torrential rills slowed down to incessant blips. Leaves began to pale and rustle and fall, and crispen and crackle. The five finger-like projections of the *chinar* curled inwards like fists, breaking into pieces if children tried to open them.

It was a time when wilting trees bared themselves to the world, unravelling traces of what the summer had done to them. And one would miss the birds that warbled their sweet music from the branches of the plum trees the whole summer.

On one of those autumnal days, Imran woke up early to prepare for his term test at school. Still unsteady from sleep, he yawned and lunged at his notebook, mugging up answers, swaying and swinging himself back and forth during the act. He hated having to cram answers and notes, for he was not comfortable with the way teachers wanted students to learn. He wanted to give his own version about things he had understood, in his own words. His arguments and persistent questions would irritate the teachers at his school. He had his own analysis of why and how prisms refracted light. He couldn't comprehend why Mrs Raazdaan, his science teacher, had not believed that both diamonds and coal were forms of carbon before she actually read it in the textbook. And another time, when Imran told her that the chemical name of water, according to a reference book in the rarely used school library, was dihydrogen monoxide, she ordered him out of the class. 'Don't disturb my lecture with your out-of-the-syllabus scraps to impress your classmates,' she had said angrily.

He didn't stop, though. He had an extra bit of information for Mrs Raazdaan in Physics: that besides an electromagnetic radiation, light, according to many other theories, had particle, wave and quantum natures as well. Imran remembered, from one of his Friday sermons, the Imam had said that God was also 'light'; He'd called Himself the light of the heavens and the earth.

Ab Jaan slurped tea from his porcelain cup and looked at Imran from the corner of his eye.

'What are you studying?' he asked him.

'Ab Jaan, the teacher is going to give us a test on Shakespeare's *The Tempest* today,' Imran said sleepily, his face crinkled from sleep.

'So why do you do it this way? Rote-learning? You do it with your other subjects too? With Mathematics too?' Ab Jaan asked.

'Almost,' said Imran.

'Almost? And with History too?'

'Almost.'

'And how will you understand and remember the history then?'

Imran looked emptily at him. 'Yes, Ab Jaan, you must come some day and talk to the principal about that. The other day our History teacher Mrs Teja Thussu tweaked my ear when I asked her a simple question…'

'Why? What?' Ab Jaan narrowed his eyes, three parallel lines creasing his forehead.

'I asked her why we were never taught the history of Kashmir. How can one study about Mesopotamia and Indus Valley and Harappa and this and that civilization but not a bit about the place one hails from?'

'And she tweaked your ear for that?'

'Indeed.'

'Pathetic. How dare she! And what did you think then?'

'Then I thought Kashmir had no real history, otherwise I would not have been punished.'

Ab Jaan sniggered. 'Until we stop oppressing ourselves others will never stop oppressing us. Remember this. Mark my words... Everything has a history. And we have a firm history. Our own history. Except the fact that it has never seen the light of day.'

'But my friends say it is not in our syllabus.'

'Because some people don't want it to be there. Not a bit of it. They don't want us to know ourselves. They don't want us to learn about who we are.'

'Then what do we do, Ab Jaan?'

'We have to indulge in alternate education… Read besides your school curriculum. I have an old copy of *Kashmakash*. Let me get it bound. I will get my reading glasses fixed and read you from it. *Filhaal*, for the time being, you prepare for the test,' Ab Jaan said, smiling.

Imran began swerving back and forth once again, committing Ferdinand, Miranda and Prospero to his memory.

'Ferdinand is lifting logs for Prospero. Ferdinand is lifting… lifting…umm...lifting…logs for Prospero…logs for Prosperooo… Prosperooo…Prospero! This doesn't bother him unduly, because, as Ferdinand puts it, his labours will lead to richer ends, the heart of Miranda:

"*There be some sports are painful, and their labour*
Delight in them sets off: some kinds of baseness
Are nobly undergone, and most poor matters
Point to rich ends."'

'Imran Jaana, drop some hay for the cows,' Haleema called out.

He shut the notebook and held it in one hand, walking out towards the cowshed, tumbling on one thing or the other on the way. Now and then he closed the notebook and repeated lines from memory: 'Ferdinand knows his work is hard, knows his work is hard…knows his work is hard, but the thought of Miranda gives him strength:

"*This my mean task*
Would be as heavy to me as odious, but
The mistress, which I serve quickens what's dead
And makes my labours pleasures: O, she is
Ten times more gentle than her father's crabbed,
And he is composed of harshness."'

Imran groped for hay at the foot of the stairs beside the cowshed's wall. Then he opened the tin door of the cowshed with a slight butt of the head. The older cow stood up and swished her tail. He smoothly rumpled her thigh while rapt in his notebook, until the cow lashed his hand with her tail and brought him back.

'Ferdinand is aware that the sight of Miranda's love (for Ferdinand) working so hard saddens Miranda (Line 10-12), but his thoughts of Miranda inspire him to go on:

"*But these sweet thoughts do even refresh my labours.*"'

When Imran began to walk back towards the house, he noticed some movement, some rustling noise, from the farther end of the orchard. Calmly, he went down the slope of the land. Hiding himself, he saw a line of a dozen or more, he couldn't say for sure, young men in *pherans,* windbreakers or long anoraks and baggy pants, in high-ankle powder-blue Warrior runners or Force-10 shoes, with medium-long wavy hairstyles and long or short oiled beards, crossing into the orchard. Thistle seeds clung to their clothes. All bore new Kalashnikovs that slung down their shoulders. Some of them wore sleeveless ammunition jackets with many pockets or pouches over their *pherans*. One among them pulled up the fence's barbwire for his companions to clamber through. He stood there holding the barbwire until the last man walked through. Imran recognized him: Imran Bhat. Shafiqa's older son.

The young men regrouped and walked like soldiers now, with a slow, careful, queued gait. Imran remained hidden behind the waist-high weeds, watching them with great curiosity, till they crossed the land and walked out the other side of the orchard.

The men fascinated Imran. His heart pounded so loudly that he could almost hear it. He imagined himself with a similar Kalashnikov, walking in a similar measured gait in someone's garden. *The Tempest* struck back. He tried to remember the lines but the scene he had just witnessed interfered with his learning. He lost track of his memory, and for sometime became oblivious of his being. Then he began again: 'Miranda tells Ferdinand to sit down...to sit down...sit down…she will "bear" or carry his logs for a while. Ferdinand, ever the noble gentleman, refuses Miranda's kind offer, telling her,

"*No, precious creature;*
I had rather crack my sinews, break my back,
Than you should such dishonour undergo,
While I sit lazy by."

(No precious creature…I would rather break my back than see you dishonoured by carrying logs…while I sit idly by.)'

Ab Jaan and Haleema listened to Imran in awe.

'It must be none other than Imran Bhat, yes…' Ab Jaan declared. 'It's he who has guided these other fellows…he must have told them that the orchard is a safe passage to cross over to the other side of the neighbourhood…I have heard he is the Natipora area commander for JKLF. What if the army comes to know about these boys, crossing our lands…We will be buried along with them…

'Don't let this cloud your mind. Leave for school immediately. Try not to think of it. And *never*,' Ab Jaan raised his voice now, '*never* tell anyone about it. Do you hear me?'

'Yes, Ab Jaan. I won't,' Imran promised.

'Yes. Now leave.'

The asphalt road that ran through Natipora, where all the processions roared, was visible from their rooftop. Imran would peer through the boughs from the rooftop at the endless number of people, swarming, shouting, halting and advancing, sloganeering. All the lanes, streets and alleyways would be packed.

One morning, he gingerly sneaked out a back window and ran to the road. A sea of *pheran*-wearing people from the neighbourhood already flanked it, waving at the passing procession, hurling packets of juice and biscuits at the shroud-clad marchers, who stood on top of snailing trucks and buses shouting slogans, their cheeks flushed, their eyes bloodshot. Numerous green flags fluttered on the vehicles. Imran nudged his way through the crowd to the front. Everybody around him repeated the slogan the procession was shouting. The words began to form on his lips too: *Azaadi*!

The only sound in the air!

He puckered his lips and sent a succession of flying kisses to the procession. People hardly noticed him. The few who did reciprocated with smiles. Imran threw a clenched fist in the *Azaadi*-thick air and imitated whatever the others shouted. Some young boys made V's with their fingers and pointed at him, expecting him to imitate them.

That year, the winter was more dismal than ever. Days began with a prickly drizzle, but the spray soon thickened, greyed and hardened into a heavy blizzard.

Early one chilly morning, Ab Jaan came to the kitchen and announced to Haleema and Imran, 'I have to go... They are marching to Chrar today.' He hurriedly had a cup of *nuun chai*, the quick sips of the scalding liquid burning his palate, slipped into his grey tweed *pheran*, wrapping his Angora muffler around his neck, and put on his favourite woollen bobble cap. He spoke through his muffler to Imran, instructing him on the chores for the day. He wiped the thin film of dust from the seat of his bicycle with his *pheran* and pedalled off.

At Natipora crossing a kilometre away, he joined a cavalcade of marchers rallying towards Chrar-e-Sharif, to the shrine of Sheikh Noor-u-din Wali, patron saint of Kashmir. A dense traffic of vehicles, hoisting small triangular green flags on their bumpers, plied sluggishly on the road, interspersing with an ocean of humanity. People climbed their roofs and walls to boost the morale of the masses.

The traffic jammed and honked and proceeded at intervals. Trains of various vehicles, bumper to bonnet, were smothered by men of all ages. They hung from the backs of buses. Many dangled out the windows. Young boys stood on the roofs of the buses, initiating a rallying cry for others who sat crammed around them.

All this time, it snowed and rained and snowed and rained and snowed. Wipers danced on the windscreens, swish swish, as snowflakes pup-pupped harder on glass. The swelling procession made it impossible for many to reach Chrar. Ab Jaan decided to leave his bicycle behind with anyone he knew along the way. He, like many others, waited for hours to move ahead, and when the procession did not seem like it would move further and the snow did not seem to stop, he decided to return.

Ab Jaan reached home with his *pheran* drenched in rain and snow in the pitch black of night. Ice crystals studded his head and shoulders, sparkling in the lantern's light. His *pheran* smelt of winter chill, a chill that had rendered his hands lifeless. He ate steaming hot rice with collards for dinner, letting his fingertips warm up by leaving them in the hot rice.

An endless curfew followed. The government announced shoot-at-sight orders for anyone who defied the curfew.

People scurried into Ab Jaan's *waan* from the backdoor, to buy milk, biscuits, pulses, onions and candles. And young boys came for cigarettes. Ab Jaan would sit at the door, noting down the demands of the jostling customers. Then, with a candle in one hand, he would grope along the dark shelves to find the things they had asked for, hot wax dripping on his fingers. *What will happen if the curfew prolongs and my stock runs out*? he thought. Ab Jaan emptied a half sack of onions with some kidney beans and a whole shelf of biscuits into a big nylon bag. 'This is all I could save from the shop for us,' Ab Jaan told Haleema. 'All the local shopkeepers have shut even their backdoors. I couldn't help seeing people upset.'

'This curfew doesn't seem to end. The governor wants us to starve and die in our homes,' Haleema said.

'Yes. And when I thought of you and Imran, I turned selfish, as selfish as the head of a family should be in such crises. Nothing is left at the shop now,' Ab Jaan said sadly.

'Come here, let me show you something,' he said to Haleema, rubbing his eyes, looking through the window and pointing at the empty road. Imran followed them. 'Look,' Ab Jaan insisted, 'do you see any hope that this will end?'

On the road, troops wearing long white military boots and fur-lined olive-green camo jackets were squatting or standing and jerking their tired legs, their machine guns propped up and straining. 'Do you see any hope?' Ab Jaan repeated.

For three consecutive days, the Joo family ate cooked onions with boiled rice. When the beans too ran out, only the rice was left. They began boiling the rice with a mixture of salt and chilli powder. Late that night, Radio Kashmir's last news bulletin of the day briefly announced a one-hour respite from the next day's curfew. In addition to the *isha*, the last prayer of the day, Ab Jaan offered two more *naful* prayers, thanking God.

The insurgency spread everywhere. Schoolchildren took to sketching Kalashnikovs, Chinese pistols, grenades, bullets and masked men on the back of their notebooks. No longer were flowers and fruits drawn.

All through the long, cold, grey days of the curfew, Imran longed for school. Education became imaginative. His classmates had begun private tuitions at home. There was no way for Imran to conduct experiments in his school's laboratory, so he would imagine sodium reacting with chlorine to form sodium chloride. He had no idea what sodium or chlorine actually looked like. He simply mugged the formula:

$$Na + Cl \rightarrow NaCl$$

The specimens in the school laboratories rotted in their phials. Dust powdered test tubes and flasks. Fungi smothered the specimen jars like velvet.

The abandoned houses in the neighbourhood became an ideal place for a new hide-and-seek game for the children: 'Militant-Military'. All other games now appeared obsolete. All one needed to do to kill one's enemy was to train the wooden gun, give it a little jerk and make a *ttaakh-ttaakh* sound. Imran always chose to become a 'militant', and with his wooden gun he would suddenly ambush a 'patrolling party' and then run away to hide in an empty Pandit house, and wait to be spotted and killed or be picked up by the 'military'.

On one occasion, Imran hid in the house that had belonged to the Tickoos, his neighbours. He waited to startle the 'military'. When he felt he had waited too long for his friends, he began to survey the house. Lint littered the floors, and fleas had begun to dwell in the roughly stacked mattresses, pillows, quilts and bedspreads in a wardrobe. The mildewed naked walls of the rooms bore novel, neat squarish patches where the family pictures had been put up. The sofa in the drawing room was in disarray, its chintz upholstery ripped apart, the coir and springs popping out. Imran noticed that the switchboxes had been gouged out from the walls. The batten bases running between the switchboxes and bulbs were stripped of their insulated copper wires. Crockery sat shattered on a countertop in the kitchen. Worm-ridden flour rotted on another shelf. The bathrooms, sinks and washbasins were parched and grimy, their taps missing.

Upstairs, on the unfurnished cement floor of a room, Imran found a satchel. He frisked its pockets, but it was empty except for torn bits of paper at its bottom. It smelt of stale books. Then, in one of the smaller outer pockets, he found a math notebook wrapped in brown paper. Suddenly, a short, strange noise startled him. Imran took it for some animals fighting, perhaps cats, in the attic. He dropped the bag and quietly sneaked out of the house with the notebook under his arm. He found the 'military' boys who had come searching for him. Imran pounced over them from behind and 'killed' them all.

Once back home, Imran riffled through the notebook's pages. One of the pages had been folded to form an arrow as a bookmark to separate the section for geometry. There were neatly drawn diagrams in pencil and some half-solved algebraic equations in the last section of the notebook before it finally faded into several blank pages.

6

The first attack

The next year, Kashmir was shut down for two hundred and seventy days.

One evening, while Imran was playing cricket on the streets with the neighbourhood kids, he saw the owner of the Tickoo house come into the street escorted by a contingent of troops. He was probably coming to collect whatever had been left behind.

Some of the troops stood guard at the gate of the house while others helped the owner load the things into the back of a one-tonne truck: a walnut-wood bedstead with a matching chest; the old, white refrigerator dotted with stickers; a gas stove; and garlands of dry, shrunken turnip slices.

And then, suddenly, gunfire tore the still air. Two insurgents attacked the contingent from two alleys – the first attack on the army in Natipora. Kalashnikovs boomed, tossing off their bronze cartridges into the air. It was unsafe to cross the road and go towards his orchard, so Imran broke into a run and sprinted towards another neighbourhood. All the other boys who were playing cricket with him immediately dispersed and ran for their lives. A broken plastic chair that doubled as the wicket remained in the crossfire, in the middle of the deserted road. A bat idled in the crease. A tennis ball remained near a *kaanger* that marked the wicket on the non-striker's end.

The gunfire continued to roll. Everybody ducked, dodged, scampered and sprinted. Scrambled *kaangers*, coal, embers, ash and stray shoes punctuated the road after them. A volley of bullets pierced the truck driver's throat. The vehicle careened and rammed into a telegraph pole, running over a Sikh trooper in the process.

Ab Jaan heard the gunfire and rolled down the shutter of his *waan*. He did not even lock it. The only safe way home was through a backstreet. He slunk through the lane and managed to reach home, desperately locking the wooden gate from the outside; then he clambered over the compound wall and jumped into his lawn.

After the two attackers fled, the troops, with no one around to avenge for the damage, dragged the Tickoo man out of the truck and began to beat him severely. They jettisoned his things into a pile on the road and set it on fire. The man scurried for his life into another lane and sought refuge in Shafiqa's house. Within minutes countless troops began to swarm the spot.

Once it was dark, there was a power cut in the neighbourhood. After the incident, most people abandoned their houses and ran off to other neighbourhoods. Those trapped in their homes or those who couldn't flee would face the consequences of staying behind. The angry troops began to indiscriminately beat those trapped inside their homes. They sprinkled gunpowder over the shops and houses on either side of the road and set them on fire.

Haleema and Ab Jaan couldn't run away. Ab Jaan had locked the wooden gate from the outside to give an impression that the Joo family had fled. But Imran hadn't still returned. *What had happened to him?* Ab Jaan and Haleema grew uneasy and full of evil premonitions. As it grew darker and scarier, they ran upstairs into a room that overlooked the road, carefully parting the curtains a little to see what was happening outside. They saw troops burning the chicken coops outside the butcher's shop. They watched the dancing flames and heard the troops hurl invectives loudly and wildly. They heard the slamming of doors and the shattering of glass and the screams of young boys pleading for mercy.

'Where did they escape?' they heard a trooper ask the boys they were beating up.

'Sir, we don't know, sir,' the trembling voices replied.

The army pulled their *pherans* over their heads and shoved them one by one into the truck.

Ab Jaan asked Haleema to go downstairs. He feared the troops would hear her cough if they came near the house.

Within no time a reinforcement contingent of the army arrived with giant floodlights, the powerful beams of which almost reached the moon and lit up the entire neighbourhood in blinding white light. When the troops reached the wooden gate of the Joo house and found it locked from the outside, they shone a torch on the house and panned it along the windows, the light licking the façade.

Hiding in one of the rooms, Haleema crouched under a thick creel blanket, numbing herself so much that her legs began to tingle. The prickling sensation changed into a dead feeling. She lifted her right leg to relieve the left one. It felt heavy, cold and lifeless. She pinched it but it didn't hurt. She turned and lay face down, and tried to silence her breath by biting on a corner of her scarf.

Ab Jaan anticipated the troops would fling the gate open and break into the house. He began to pray that nothing creaked or tinkled or chimed. The troops began to probe the lock. Groping his way in the darkness, Ab Jaan tiptoed to his prayer room. He picked up his Quran from the niche and hugged it tightly. Tears streamed down his wrinkled cheeks and disappeared into his grizzled, short beard.

Outside, a trooper grumbled and rapped hard on the door with his rifle butt. Ab Jaan abruptly wetted his pyjamas. Warm urine trickled down his legs and he fainted and fell down.

He woke up with the Quran still on his chest. He felt his body, touching each part to ascertain the tangibility of his physicality. He sensed himself with his quivering fingers, affirming whether the solidity of his existence had translated into something that, he thought, could feel like air. He checked himself for bullets and the moistness of blood but only felt the wetness of his pyjamas. He stood up and staggered towards the curtains. The troops were gone and now the dogs were barking loudly. It was no less than a miracle that the troops had spared them. *Why*? He did not know. He only kept thanking God.

Ab Jaan dizzily descended the wooden flight of stairs and found Haleema gilded in a film of sweat, huffing. He lifted the blanket off her face. She was breathing the way she snored. He slipped his hand under her scruff and pitched her head up. Then he pumped the inhaler thrice into her mouth.

'They are gone,' Ab Jaan mumbled. 'Don't worry Haleemai, they are gone. Breathe…long…longer… Good!'

'Imran?' she whimpered, her breath still hoarse.

'He will be safe, Insha'Allah. Don't worry about him. Believe me, he will be safe,' Ab Jaan cooed, slowly clearing his dry throat.

If he returns in the night they will pounce on him, Haleema thought. She tried to shake the inevitable thoughts off her mind, lying awake throughout the night.

At dawn, Natipora sluggishly came back to life. People started checking their courtyards for stray cartridges or misplaced bullets. Haleema and Ab Jaan stonily surveyed for Imran.

Imran emerged a few hours later. Haleema felt breathless while hugging him.

She hugged him tight; he felt her heart pounding against his chest. 'I am here now,' Imran assured her. She raised her hand to slap him but withdrew it midway. She wanted to ask him a dozen questions at once: Where had he been? How had he escaped? But asking those questions now, she felt, was futile.

She caressed his arms and face to confirm he was all right.

Then Ab Jaan held Imran in the crook of his arm and kissed his face all over.

Imran explained everything. How he had escaped to another locality he had hardly been to. How difficult, while running randomly in desperation, it had been to decide where he should have actually gone. How he had made it to a house where nobody knew him. How he first briefed and later described everything to the people in that house, huffing and trembling. How he was treated there courteously.

How he passed the night alternating between sleep and waiting for the dawn to break. Imagining worst things about Ab Jaan and his Ammi. He kept turning under his blanket, straining his ears to tell the noise of the night from the snoring of the old man whose room it was.

Clouds of odorous smoke billowed out from under the two iron channels where the shutter of Ab Jaan's *waan* fit. Not presuming it to be very hot, Ab Jaan singed his fingers when he touched the shutter. The paint on the signboard above the shop was blistered, the brightly lettered sign 'GR JOO GENERAL STORE' beginning to flake off. He slipped a giant claw hammer under the shutter to jimmy it and pry it open.

The shop was full of sourly pungent smoke. The bars of soap stacked on one of the shelves had melted; the packets of salt and detergent had charred. Sooted, shattered glassware was strewn all over. The cigarettes and biscuits were a smoking ash of their original forms. Candles on another shelf had melted and fused with scorched pencils and partially seared stationery. Shampoo bottles had warped into strange plastic sculptures. Toothpaste tubes, toothbrushes and pens had twisted beyond recognition. The candy had melted, along with their glass jars. There was nothing on the wire loop hanger fixed to the ceiling in front of the shop. The sultry loose change that he collected in a steel bowl inside the drawer of the counter was darkly mottled. Hopeless, the Joos sat in silent mourning.

The next morning, a patrolling party led by a Major Aman Lal Kushwaha began to search the houses. Almost all the men in the neighbourhood received their share of beating in turns. The army was still angry over the attack.

From their room upstairs, the Joo family furtively looked at the beatings. Haleema rubbed her hands together in fear, while Ab Jaan's face darkened. As the troops came closer to their house, he became jittery with anger and fear. Imran's mouth was dry with fear.

The army called out the male members once they were outside the gate. Ab Jaan decided to go and open the gate but Haleema didn't let him. 'Don't worry, I will be all right,' Ab Jaan assured her darkly. No sooner had he opened the wooden gate than he found Major Aman Lal Kushwaha facing him.

The major had small eyes that were stacked deep into his inscrutable, sallow face.

'Where did you hide them?' the irate major asked, shoving Ab Jaan to the ground.

'Whom?' Ab Jaan said.

He hit Ab Jaan hard on the arm with his rifle.

'Don't lie. All you sisterfucking Kashmiris lie! You know you lie. Tell me where did they go? Sisterfucker, your orchard is so vast and dense…Tell me, or I'll shoot you right here,' Kushwaha warned.

Haleema ran down and shielded Ab Jaan, crying and begging the major to let them go. Imran watched mistily, clinging to Haleema, clutching her *pheran* tightly, freezing with fear.

'We don't know anything. Please don't beat him, *balaai lagai*,' Haleema pleaded.

'Take him aside,' Kushwaha ordered his men, pointing towards Ab Jaan. Then he slapped Imran.

'What is this? You beat everyone. There are civilians in this locality, yet you burn down our shops, you snatch away our living and now you are torturing us. Don't you have any shame?' Ab Jaan argued bravely, yet trembling.

'Shut up or I'll kill you!' Kushwaha threatened.

'Ab Jaan, please don't argue with them! Please!' Haleema pleaded, wringing her hands.

Ab Jaan didn't budge.

'Kill me, go ahead, I don't want to live in a world where I have to live with inhuman people like you,' Ab Jaan dared, his brown eyes glinting with confidence.

'Enough!' Kushwaha held Ab Jaan by his collar and dragged him towards the large mortar beside the small ornamental lawn in front of the house. Two troops held Haleema and Imran back. Haleema screamed for help. '*Kuni kahn chhu na*? Anybody? Help! Please don't kill him! *Please*!' She screeched.

Three bullets were pumped into Ab Jaan. One in the neck. One in the heart. One in the stomach. The rapid staccato startled the birds in the plum trees.

'Sisterfucker!' Kushwaha said after killing Ab Jaan, the fevered barrel of his rifle still smoking.

Haleema frenetically slapped her face and her chest and pulled her hair. Blood began to gurgle out of Ab Jaan's throat. She fainted. The entire neighbourhood was now watching from their rooftops, verandahs and windows. Men and boys jumped off and rushed to help. Major Kushwaha cocked his gun. His men followed and pointed their guns at the people who tried to come towards the Joos. Women of the neighbourhood wailed from their rooftops and verandahs and pummelled their chests.

The major fired some warning shots. 'No one will come here. Whoever does shall meet the same fate!' he announced.

Imran had frozen in the shock. After some time, an old woman mustered enough courage to pull Haleema and Imran away. She tried to go towards where Ab Jaan lay but the troops pushed her backwards. She dragged Imran and Haleema to her own lawn. Some boys jumped off their walls and helped her. Some of them took Imran away and consoled him passionately. People crowded around Haleema and rubbed her feet first. They opened a little gap in her sternly shut mouth and poured water into it from a steel tumbler.

Another old woman went hurtling through the column of troops. 'Let me give some water to him. He is dying. What kind of people are you? Don't you have any pity?' she begged Major Kushwaha.

'No, he doesn't need it,' the major grumbled.

The woman cursed him in Kashmiri but Kushwaha didn't react.

'At least let us drape his body. We can't bear looking at him like this,' the Imam requested.

'No, let everyone see this! See what happens when you rebel against us,' Kushwaha said, and walked away.

A pool of blood gleamed in the dull sun near Ab Jaan's body. His throat was scabbed. His eyes remained open and his mouth agape. Blood had started to congeal around the charred bullet holes on his *pheran*.

Once the troops withdrew, neighbours put the body on a stretcher borrowed from the mosque and placed it on the Joo verandah, covering it with a blanket. The rumble of mourning began to emanate from everywhere. A dozen young boys ringed around the body to guard it. There was a stampede each time anyone wanted to see Ab Jaan for the last time. The boys pushed and nudged and beat people who tried to overwhelm them. One of the boys announced, 'Okay! Okay! We will elevate him a little so that all are able to see him. But please don't come close, please, please! Stay back and make some way. Stay back, please. For God's sake, please stay back.'

They lifted Ab Jaan's lifeless head and drew the blanket a little. The spectacle of the bloodless, pale face sent the crowd bawling. Everyone – men, women, children and the aged – burst out into congregational sobs. As the boys elevated the body a little more, the chaotic hum picked up further. Women began to slap their chests. Men wept like women. And women like mad men.

Ab Jaan was now as pale as butter.

All this while, the women tried to prevent Haleema from hurting herself. She was conscious now and in shock. She wanted the women to tell her Ab Jaan was still alive. 'Please don't cry. My Ab Jaan is alive. Isn't he? Isn't he? *He is alive.* Why are you all crying?' she requested the women. Her tears had dried. The skin beneath her throat was red from chest-thumping. Her cheeks had the imprints of her own slaps. Her hair fell loose over her face. She laughed, and then abruptly ran towards a wall barefooted to bang her head. The women rushed to stop her. She rubbed her heels against the earth. Her shalwar slipped from under her feet. She tried to wrest herself away from the women who came to help her.

The boys and some elders were trying their best to calm Imran down.

Someone brought a bier from the mosque and put it on the verandah. Its lid was like a Kashmiri tin roof. An A-shaped bier. They covered the body in a white sheet. Draped in the white shroud, Ab Jaan's body looked taller than it actually was. The boys lifted the lid of the coffin and carefully placed the body inside it. The Imam took out a green satin pall from a plastic bag and draped it over the tin lid of the coffin. The pall was dotted with glittering golden Arabic calligraphy. The boys angled the body parallel to the direction of the Kaaba in Mecca, and the Imam began his funeral prayers.

Once the prayers were over, the Imam and three other boys lifted the coffin and placed it on their shoulders. Imran still couldn't believe what was happening.

The funeral procession passed through the main road. Thousands of men followed, chanting slogans:

Assalaam! *Assalaam*!
Ae shaheed assalaam!
Aaj teri maut pe ro raha hai yeh jahan!
Ro rahi hai yeh zameen, ro raha hai aasmaan!

The procession passed slowly. Imran led the pallbearers now, his right shoulder under the front left corner of the bier. Children who would get free toffees from Ab Jaan now walked in his funeral procession, crying and snivelling. Windows, roofs, walls and verandahs were lined with puzzled, shocked and wailing women and men. Ab Jaan's death was the first of its kind in Natipora. At one house, an old woman struggled to peer out of her window, which bore perforated translucent plastic sheets instead of panes. She cut a head-sized hole in the plastic sheet of one section, craning her neck out through it. When the funeral reached under her window, she cut another hole and showered fistfuls of toffees and almonds all over the coffin.

In the ancestral Joo graveyard, the local undertaker had readied the grave. The men removed Ab Jaan's shroud-draped body from the bier and lowered it into the vault dug into the right side of the rectangular pit. Then they shut the vault with slabs of wood and threw the earth back into the pit until it became a mound.

That night, the Joo house resounded with wails underneath the dark starry sky. The whole orchard was full of mourners. The Joos' kith and kin had already turned up. Amid the mourners, conscious yet unsettling and inconsolable, Haleema was reclining against the lap of Shafiqa. She had a spread of turmeric pasted on her forehead to ward off a headache. Shafiqa held Haleema's head, while Haleema was crooning a dirge like a wedding madrigal, refusing to believe what had happened:

'I don't believe this, my father isn't dead! Isn't this a lie, my father? Your death has battered me, my father!'

The boys, huddled in small groups, sat outside, discussing everything that had happened. A bespectacled young man in a blue pullover and black baggy pants listened intently. He had a serious look about himself: a broad forehead, a straight nose and a very short, boxed beard. He carried a small backpack, from which he took out a pen and held it between his teeth while unhitching the string from the bag. Then he fished out a mini-recorder and a notepad from it. Noticing him, the boys snapped their conversation and fell quiet. The man looked unfamiliar to them. A neighbourhood elder asked him who he was.

'*Assalaam-u-Alaiqum*! I am your friend. My name is Izhar Ahmad. I am from the BBC,' the young man introduced himself.

Upon hearing 'the BBC', the boys began a side conversation. They were happy to see the person who would give their news on the radio station all of them attentively listened to.

'I was here in Natipora the whole day, recording the tragedy. I went around to the burial too. Just need some more details from you, if you are willing, to substantiate the news. The truth needs to be confirmed, as you know,' he said.

Inside the Joo household, the wails continued to erupt.

Two weeks after Ab Jaan died, Shafiqa's house was raided. The troops beat her elderly husband and threw their belongings, utensils, rice and flour onto the street, setting them on fire. They threatened Shafiqa that if her sons did not surrender they would take Rukhsana, her daughter, away.

A month later, Shafiqa's younger son, Shaheen Bhat, and some other insurgents were caught from a hideout in downtown Srinagar. Imran Bhat, Shaheen's older brother, still remained underground.

7

The raid

Imran's exams did not go as well as he had expected. Ab Jaan's death weighed heavily on his mind. He knew Ab Jaan would probably have surprised him with something more than a set of new textbooks this time, maybe a new bicycle or even a wristwatch. He would lie on his back, awake till late, and stare at the ceiling, picturing Ab Jaan's grave that by now was a mound of earth surrounded by butterfly-thronged irises with their clumps of long knife-like leaves. Suddenly, a spurt of frissons would run through his body and fill him with outrage and vengeance.

Late one night, when Imran had just overcome his sleeplessness, a flurry of noise woke him up. His heart quickened. He propped himself up from under his warm quilt and then sat upright against the cold wall to pay attention to the noise of the terrible dark of his room. There were troops outside, knocking over whatever fell in their way, hollering a name: *Imran*! Befuddled and jittery, Imran quickly tried to connect in his mind as to what could have possibly brought the men to hound him. *Him*?

He shuddered, and could now hear his heart thumping wildly. He could feel his throat getting parched. He gingerly groped his way to the next room where Haleema, too, was stethoscopically straining her ears to listen to the din. Imran's voice grew husky to call Haleema.

'Come in, Imran,' she murmured, tremblingly. 'Stay put, *zuv wandai*.'

She put his head in her lap and patted his shivering head gently.

'Perhaps they are actually looking for Imran Bhat. Perhaps they are mistaken.'

'Perhaps,' Imran responded.

They could now hear the troops scrubbing their shoes; the sounds grew louder and louder as the men approached the main door. Then, the moment they dreaded: someone rapped on the main door. It was followed by a horrible call from a spooky voice: 'Everyone, come out!'

Trembling, Haleema swiftly flung her tatty maroon shawl about herself and quaveringly mustered to respond, 'But what do you want, sir? Both of us are alone here, my son and I.' She stammered in fear but tried to sound intact.

'No questions! Open the door before we break in,' the groaning voice preceded a harder knock on the door.

Inside Haleema's room, in the dread and uncertainty, Imran shrivelled, waiting for her to open the door. He desperately wore his *pheran* over his loose, oversized, saggy-necked mint-green inner. He could taste his bile now.

As Haleema unbolted the door, a burly, moustached trooper pushed her aside, forcing his way in. A row of uniformed men frantically burst in behind him. A bunch of them ran upstairs. Major Kushwaha followed, his fearsome whiskers just beginning to join his sideburns. He stomped about the house and then walked into the room where Imran had been cowering in horror. As he stepped in, Imran fretfully slunk out the window he had unbolted in advance. The troops who had been left outside in the dark frontyard caught hold of him by the neck of his *pheran*. Imran uttered a shrill shriek. 'Ammi! Save me!'

'Nice boy. Come on,' Major Kushwaha said as if he was luring a kid with toffee.

Haleema ran out, frustrated with fear, sobbing, and tried to wriggle Imran out of the crook of the trooper's arm.

'He is my only son, sir! He…' Haleema was desperate.

'Why did you run?' the major interrupted her.

'Nnn…' Imran sputtered and swallowed. Small droplets of sweat beaded his fuzzy upper lip and under the traces of his fine teenage beard, now growing only along his chin and under his temples.

'Get the cat,' Major Kushwaha ordered his men, referring to their informant.

The troops brought out a tall boy from one of their jeeps. He wore an oversized khaki trench coat, the coat so long that it swept the earth behind him as he walked. He hid his hands in its cuffs. His face was masked with a black cloth and only his thin eyes were visible.

He nodded once.

'Here he is then,' Kushwaha said. 'Formalities over.'

'He is innocent, sir!' Haleema bawled.

'Take him, Manoj!' Kushwaha barked at one of his men.

'You killed my father! Leave me someone to live with! How could you be so cruel?' Haleema begged the inscrutable Kushwaha.

Outside the flimsy wooden gate, the olive-green jeeps began to chug. Imran cried and screamed impulsively. He strove to break free from the trooper's hold, but they continued to drag him towards one of the jeeps. His teeth clattered from the cold and fear.

'Water!' he screamed.

Haleema tightly clasped Imran's hand and grappled with it; she was dragged with him as they wrested him away. Her shawl fell off. Her plastic sandals slipped out. The cow mooed in panic from its shed. It kicked out at the walls of the shed. The chickens raised an alarm from their hutch. By now Haleema's neighbours were awake and peering out the windows of their blacked-out homes.

'What is his crime? What has he done? You are mistaken! You know you are mistaken! Why do you do this to me?' Haleema pleaded.

'Ssshhh!' Major Kushwaha said.

'He is a small child! Don't you see?' she wailed.

She picked up her shawl and spread it at his feet.

'I beg you, *balaai lagai*, he is innocent!' she reiterated effusively.

'We have to ask him a couple of questions. He will be back in a jiffy,' Kushwaha said, the voice now sounding like a fox's.

'Please, brother, I have no one except him. Leave him for God's sake!' She tugged at the trooper's hand, the one who was holding Imran. He returned her tears with callous indifference.

'*Kuni kahn chhu na khuadaaya*!' she screamed out. 'Anybody, please help, for God's sake!'

The trooper bundled Imran into the Gypsy and hastily leapt behind him. He stood there, holding on to the railing of the Gypsy's roof. Haleema ran in front of the vehicle and knelt in front of its bonnet, breathing hard, begging and crying for Imran's release. A trooper dragged her aside and the Gypsy picked up speed.

Haleema chased the Gypsy until it vanished in the thick blanket of darkness.

Amm, the local baker, was the first neighbour to come out. He shouted and called the others out.

Haleema collapsed on the dirt road, wailing, barefooted, bare-headed.

In a few minutes the whole neighbourhood was shaken awake. Shafiqa pulled a stupefied Haleema into her lap. '*Gaed ha kaertham, patro*! I am a perforated soul, my son,' Haleema muttered in a singsong voice. Two frozen trails of tears glistened on her cheeks.

Shafiqa wound her right arm around Haleema and lifted her up. Some other women collected Haleema's sandals and shawl.

A sixty-watt bulb on a street pole glowed biliously within the dull halo of its spiky orange light.

Shafiqa and Rukhsana sat flanking Haleema, persuasively calming her. The neighbours discussed Haleema's situation with the Imam and finally decided to wait till dawn. Everybody dispersed after that. Shafiqa and Rukhsana volunteered to stay back with Haleema. She crooned until her jaws exhausted themselves.

Haleema imagined the troops kicking Imran with their hard, white jackboots. She imagined him crying for her help – calling her name. Asking for water. *Water! I couldn't even give him a tumbler of water! But how could I?*

She imagined him rattling in the chill of a formidable army camp.

At least water.

At least, she crooned.

It was the longest night of Haleema's life. She crooned and sobbed throughout the night. Shafiqa and Rukhsana kept consoling her. Just an hour before the break of dawn, Shafiqa and Rukhsana involuntarily fell asleep. Haleema was wide awake. She could hear her house and all its things creaking in the silence of the night. A tight-lidded tin drum in the kitchen swelled out with a burp. A drop of water fell from the bathroom tap and plopped on a half-filled bucket under it. A cat skittled an old, dented aluminium pitcher on the gable in the attic. The rattle lasted. Mice began to scurry in the wooden ceiling and smuggle crumbs and leftovers to their bores.

Book II

8

Brief version/Full version

The first ray of the sun at the break of dawn lit up a hole in the coarse blanket covering the window of the room where Shafiqa, Rukhsana and Haleema were lying. The light began to grow brighter by the minute. Haleema had not slept a wink.

The room smelt of sleep and stale breath. The mosque's loudspeakers were fervently humming the post-namaaz *durood*, praises to the prophet Muhammad. Roosters began to crow but the birds were yet to chirp from the plum trees.

Haleema let her two companions sleep. Without waking them up, she crossed herself and started pacing the room, then tottered to the bathroom and washed her sleep-deprived, gummy face. Then she slipped over her fluffing blazer and wore her black plastic shoes.

It was freezing outside. The cloudy dawn looked sad and desolate. Frenzied, Haleema went straight to the Imam's house. The Imam had just returned from the *fajr namaaz*. Haleema looked weary and tired. Her hair was loose, her dupatta was wound carelessly around her head, and her eyes were swollen and moist. Her face was pale and dry, like a corpse's. The Imam noticed that Haleema had worn her *pheran* inside out. He also noticed a deep gash on her right foot. The wound had partly dried, but the bleeding hadn't stopped completely. She had injured it while chasing the Gypsy.

While the Imam's wife swaddled Haleema's foot in bandage, Haleema begged the Imam to find her son. She cried, snivelled, crooned, then wiped her nose with her dupatta. Shafiqa and Rukhsana, who had been looking for Haleema, found her pleading with the Imam. Haleema, Shafiqa and the Imam decided to go to the Saddar Police Station two kilometres away.

The pillbox bunker next to the shrine was quiet at that hour. An LMG muzzle poked out of its pigeonhole of a window. A monkey-capped trooper in the doorway sat crushing coal for the *bukhari*. Dogs, still asleep, lay cringing together in huddles, sticking their paws into each other's bellies for warmth. The road had worn out and the gravel under it had come loose. Thin glassy floes blanketed the puddles. Electric poles leaned over the road at perilous angles. High-tension wires sagged between them. The newspaper hawker was only just slipping the morning papers under the locked shutters.

The black paint on the iron gate of Saddar Police Station had begun to peel. The gate was bolted from the inside. The guard's watchtower was empty. Haleema and Shafiqa patted the gate with the flats of their palms, first gently and then harder. For a moment there was silence and no one responded. Then somebody called from the inside, 'Who is it?'

'*Ba haz chhas*, Haleema!'

Someone shuffled inside, then unbolted the gate. The scratchy squeak that the bolt issued made the Imam grit his teeth. Wrapped in a fraying tartan blanket, a tall police constable with matted, tousled hair and medium-length beard appeared groggily from behind the gate.

'Yes? Tell me what is it?' he asked.

'Last night the army burst in…' Haleema stated in a tremor-ridden voice, coughing and weeping. The phlegm in her throat knotted her voice. The cough didn't stop. It led to another bout of endless coughing. Shafiqa and the Imam narrated the rest of her story to the constable.

'Relax. Come inside,' the constable said sympathetically.

He ushered them into the police station, took them into a poorly lit room and made them sit on wooden chairs. He brought a chilled glass of water from somewhere and offered it to Haleema. 'Have it, sister.'

'Can't drink cold water,' Haleema croaked. She fumbled the pocket of her *pheran* looking for her inhaler but realized she had left it behind. Her eyes turned moist and red with breathlessness. She began to gather her breath, and then told her story.

The other constables could be heard snoring from one section of the station. Once Haleema finished her tale, the constable stared emptily at the window of the room, the panes filled with cloudy winter light.

'It has been a long time since we filed an FIR. A long, long time. Actually, we cannot lodge an FIR against the army.' The constable spoke with a countryside dialect. 'Our job is now confined to identifying, carrying and delivering dead bodies to their families. That is the job of the police now,' he said slowly, with a tired smile behind his weighed words. 'Sister, in your case, the only way is to approach the army itself. They take everyone they pick up to their local camps.'

None of the three was convinced by the constable's remarks, but they trusted the sincerity of his words. They didn't have much of a choice but to trust him.

On their way back, at Barzalla Bridge, they saw a swarm of young boys and elders sit around something. The results of the tenth grade exams were out. A young boy sat on the bridge with a result gazette in his lap, the collar of his *pheran* pulled back, the zipper almost touching his throat. He was juggling with an overwhelming crowd.

It is Imu Ji's result today! Haleema told Shafiqa and the Imam, who then requested the boy, '*Jigra*, could you see the status of a roll number for me, please?' Haleema tried to subdue herself. The crowd grew curious at her condition and made way for the trio.

'But why are you crying? You don't even know the result yet,' the boy asked Haleema.

'I want to know my son's result. He was picked up last night.'

'Oh oh! That is very sad. Give me the roll number,' the boy asked.

'I don't know...I don't remember it. Only my son knows it.'

'Don't you worry! Give me his name and the name of his school.'

The boy flipped through the pages of the gazette, back and forth and back again.

'What name did you say?' he repeated.

'Imran. Imran Joo,' the Imam said.

The boy ran his finger down a long list of names in tiny font.

'Imran Joo, Imran Joo, Imran Joo, Imran Joo, Imran Joo,' he whispered to himself, looking for the correct name. And then stopped in the middle of the page.

'Here it is,' he read it aloud, 'Roll No. 314789, Imran Joo, Pass, Distinction, 377 marks.'

Haleema abruptly burst into tears. Shafiqa and the Imam were also surprised. They all felt helpless. The Imam held out a fifty rupee note for the boy.

'No no, nothing for you. A tenner if you have passed, twenty if it's first division or distinction – but I won't charge you anything,' the boy told Haleema.

The Imam continued to hold out the note his way and insisted that he take it. The boy resisted. The crowd collectively said, 'No. No. Let it be.'

'Okay, but take some for my sake,' Haleema said.

The boy took the note and returned forty rupees.

The Imam's grainy voice bellowed from the megaphones fixed on the wooden posts under the tin dome of the mosque: '*...have created you male and female, and appointed you races and tribes, that you may know one another, not that you may despise each other. Surely the noblest among you in the sight of God is the most God-fearing of you. God is all-knowing, all-aware...'* White, grey and dappled pigeons roosted about the dome. Then the prayer started. The Imam chanted, *Allah-o-Akbar*! His voice sliced through the frozen silence of the winter morning. It startled the birds; they flew around the dome in a maelstrom for a while before settling back in their previous spots.

Haleema passed by rows of haphazardly parked bicycles, a column of mischievous children, beggars, hundreds of shoes left outside and rice sprinkled on the steps of the mosque. She impatiently walked into the squinched foyer and peeked into the grand hall where people were whispering prayers in prostration. The Imam too was on his knees, his head digging in the alcove.

Haleema sat on one of the steps outside and waited for the namaaz to end. Those few minutes felt like hours. The Imam repeated the chants several times and the endless rows of heads prostrated in acquiescence. Someone sneezed, another person coughed, a throat cleared itself and then a flurry of sneezes, coughs and throat clearings followed once the Imam finished.

Haleema tried to pass that time watching the pigeons. One of the dappled pigeons now flitted away and swooped in the sky once before diving and perching on a power line. Then it flapped once more, fanned its wings and flew about a poplar tree, finally gliding down to the ground and beginning to peck.

Her heart palpitated heavily and a strange liquefied feeling fluxed throughout her body. It suffused and dilated to the very roots of her hair, surging and leaving her breathless. A sudden tremor in her heart said, *You have lost your son.*

The namaaz ended and people started walking out, yodelling holy words.

Frustrated, she cried out madly in front of them.

'Did you see my Imran?' she asked a *durood*-muttering woman.

'He is just young… Looks just like me,' she continued, desperately jostling through the crowds, pulling their arms and patting their backs.

'Have you seen my Imu Ji? Oh God, where is my Imran?'

She ran into the mosque and approached the Imam.

The Imam directed the mosque management committee to make an announcement. Soon a microphone blared: '*Hazraat*! This appeal is to everyone to please gather at the shrine. One of our young boys was picked up last night. Please report to the Auqaaf committee immediately.'

Gradually, young boys, elderly men and women gathered at the shrine where Haleema was already waiting.

'Don't worry, I fed the cattle,' Shafiqa told Haleema empathically. She too had come to join her.

'You all know he is my only reason to live,' Haleema told the crowd.

Everyone unanimously agreed.

Then they accompanied her to the local army camp.

The army camp was a kilometre away from Natipora, headquartered in a Pandit's sprawling abandoned house. The guard at the entrance was listening to an old Hindi song on a small radio that had been carefully balanced atop a low wall of sandbags. The transistor's tapering steel antenna stood at a slanting angle in the air. His rifle sat on his thighs. When he noticed a horde of people approaching the camp, he turned off the radio, put on his helmet, slipped its strap under his chin and slung the rifle over his shoulder, his crooked finger near the trigger.

'We are looking for a young boy. Your captain picked him up last night from Natipora – he is the only son of this lady,' the Imam told him.

'Yes, I saw major sahib bring a boy last night. But…' Before the soldier could complete his sentence, one of his colleagues emerged and interrupted him with a wink and a cough.

The Imam insisted on meeting the major.

'He is not here,' the second trooper said stiffly.

'At least give us a clue of our boy,' the Imam demanded.

'Okay, okay, you can meet Lance Naik Sharmaji, but only you,' the trooper told the Imam.

The first trooper stepped out to frisk the Imam before letting him in. When he kneeled to check the pockets of his *pheran*, he murmured quietly, 'Major has shifted your boy somewhere else.'

And then he loudly pretended to be strict, '*Chalo, chalo*! All of you wait here.'

'There is no reason meeting the Lance Naik. Follow me,' the Imam told the crowd.

He led the surprised crowd back, disclosing what the guard had whispered to him. The way the first trooper had behaved had left no doubt that he should not be believed. When the little procession reached the shrine, Haleema stopped and sat in the middle of the road. Everyone followed her. In some minutes more people joined and the crowd swelled. Young boys of the neighbourhood assembled and placed big stones and discarded tyres on the road, creating a barrier to block the traffic. 'This will attract the attention of the authorities,' the Imam said.

Initially, the troops inside the bunker at the shrine watched silently. After sometime, a trooper spoke rapidly into his sibilating, black walkie-talkie: 'Alpha Charlie Alpha Tango. Charlie One Hello! *Dharna, dharna*, Charlie One. Over!'

Minutes later, a picket of troops donning camo jackets arrived from nowhere and prowled around the crowd with rifles in one hand and freshly peeled, creamy willow sticks or bamboo canes in the other. Their olive one-tonne truck preceded them.

First, they caught hold of some of the boys by their collars and kicked their behinds repeatedly, as if a football team was rehearsing its pre-match dribble. Then they began showering volleys of expletives. '*Saala,* attempting a sit-in huh? *Saala*!' They shooed the people away and continued beating the boys. They began dismantling the blockade and beating the drivers of the vehicles that had stopped because of the obstacle.

'You didn't want to move either. You are all the same, *saalon*,' a Sikh trooper grouched, breaking a crooked willow lathi on the door of a stranded bus. All the other drivers pressed their accelerators and let their vehicles fly.

In wake of the chase, shoes, mufflers and caps littered the road.

The army whisked away a few boys and threw them one by one

into their truck. As the large vehicle drove on, the troops jumped in its rear and stood there, hanging, looking this way and that with creased faces and wide eyes.

People kept assembling at the shrine in the days that followed, marching to the local camp and protesting with Haleema. And each day they were beaten and dispersed. Meanwhile, the battalions changed at the local camp and the noble trooper who had tried to help Haleema was transferred.

'The same name, same height, same eyes, same hair and same complexion…that is how Muhammad Shafi, my neighbour, described the boy whom he had seen at the camp where his son was detained,' the Imam informed Haleema, 'maybe that boy is him… maybe it is Imran? You never know…let's go and see?'

At the army camp, inexplicably named 'Malaysia', Haleema, glowing from grief and sleeplessness, and the Imam requested – and begged – the two troopers at the gate to allow them to see Imran. After an hour of waiting and begging, they were shown into a small shadowy room with a rusty coal brazier that was not working. Three broken wooden chairs sat empty around the brazier. The room had an unbearable stench of something rotten. They squatted on the bare dirty cement floor, not willing to risk the chairs.

A major with two other troopers appeared suddenly and brusquely informed them that no boy called Imran was in the camp, and therefore, they should leave. Haleema desperately described Imran's features to the major and then showed him Imran's picture. At this, the major began to bark at Haleema. He declined to acknowledge his battalion's role in picking up anyone from Natipora, which was four kilometres away from 'Malaysia'. 'I do not know anyone called Major Aman Kushwaha.'

Haleema and the Imam got up to leave; there wasn't much else they could do. As they walked back towards the gate, they saw one of the troopers who had accompanied the major inside the room seemingly waiting to tell them something. The two slowed down to let the trooper follow them. The trooper began to mutter something while showing them out of the camp – perhaps a clue about Imran – but before they could understand what he was saying, another trooper appeared to discourage any further communication.

They waited outside the camp, expecting the trooper to show up and say something, help them with some clue. But no one came. Only armoured vehicles carrying army supplies and reinforcements entered and left the camp.

'The greatest of sufferings bring the greatest of hopes, the greatest of miseries greatest patience, and the greatest of uncertainties lead to the greatest quests,' the Imam told her on the way back home.

The Imam's gentle assurance did not satisfy Haleema. The trooper from 'Malaysia' haunted her; the abrupt termination of a conversation where she might have had more clues pained her. She continued to sit outside the camp's gates to catch a glimpse of the trooper. This continued until she was convinced a new battalion had taken over the camp.

Haleema sold her cattle to Shafiqa for ten thousand rupees, as well as her jewellery and more expensive copper utensils. The Joo house wore an empty look now. Each day, consoling neighbours would drop by, and once they left she would find herself entirely alone. She began talking to herself or to the walls. Sometimes, she would talk to the things that belonged to Imran, crying and wailing alternately. She would open the dented heirloom trunk and take out his notebooks. She would slowly run her fingers over his scribbles and feel the letters, smelling the pages while riffling through them. Again and again. She had carefully ironed and folded his school uniform – the white shirt, grey pants and red sweater – and placed them in the trunk, along with his identity card, his stationery and the badge that said I ♡

KASHMIR. She would often take his clothes out and converse with them. Converse with them and kiss them. Kiss them and sniff them for his smell. Sniff them and neatly fold them again.

Then, melancholically, she would croon a song:

Kyazi tscaa'i roodham maah-i-nam ke hilaal tai?
Doh goum pyaaraan, chhi na tsalaan malaal tai?

O crescent moon, why do you hide from me?
Sulking as you are, why have you kept me?

One morning, the first sound that struck Haleema was a faint chirping of birds. She gulped down half a dozen coloured pills and half a glass of water after each. Once done, she locked the gate and stopped for a moment to remind herself where she was headed to.

After an hour or so, she found herself at Zero Bridge, asking strangers for directions to the radio station. She approached a weary-looking man who sold fish fritters from a cart. He wiped his fingers – smeared with a pink paste of chickpea flour – with a grubby rag, as if he was going to touch something clean, and pointed to his left.

There was little traffic outside the radio station. When she tried to push the heavy cast-iron gate to enter, a trooper whistled at her from a watchtower.

'What do you want?' he asked brusquely.

'I want to see the news people,' Haleema said.

The trooper signalled to someone in the outhouse security hut. A Kashmiri man with a long flowing beard peeked out of the gate.

'Yes?' he asked her.

'I want to give the news of my son,' she briefly narrated the story of Imran's disappearance to him. By now, she had two versions of the story. A brief one, for purposes of emergency, and a full one which she used only if she had the time.

The man sat her on a bench in the lobby of the radio station.

'I need to check whether the news producer is available or not,' he told her.

As she waited there, Haleema scanned the black-and-white photographs of voice-artists from Kashmiri radio dramas on the walls. Surprisingly, they wore costumes that suited the characters in their photographs. It was not necessary to wear costumes in a medium that was blind, but it was deemed to be professional. It might have given them the feel of what they had supposed themselves to be, their characters, Haleema guessed. Elsewhere, in the gloomiest part of the lobby's cornice, beyond a lightless, enormous cut-glass chandelier and sconces on the wall, was a larger-than-life-portrait of Gandhi. He held a long staff in his hand, his head bald. A white sheet of cloth wound around his body and he looked distressed and disappointed at the same time.

The bearded man returned and walked Haleema down an endless, windowless white-walled corridor with thick screen doors cut in the walls. Large monochrome portraits of Kashmiri poets and mystics embellished the walls – Lal Ded, Habba Khatoon, Mehjoor, Azad and others.

'I can only do one thing for you. I will take you to the news producer. Rest is not in my power. I am a fourth-class employee here,' the man told her, breathing heavily while walking. He ushered Haleema into the news producer's room.

The news producer's back was turned to the entrance; he was on the phone. When he heard Haleema enter, he turned slightly and then swivelled fully. His eyes floated from Haleema to the bearded man and then back to her, while he continued to speak on the phone. He wore an ash-grey tweed jacket and a red tie with sparse white stripes. Haleema had been told he was the producer of the noon news bulletin.

'…Yes. Yes. We have carried Governor sahib's full statement. You can surely cross-check on our broadcast. Oh! Okay. Okay. Ooookay! Nice. Nice. Oookay. Okay. Bye,' he hung up and brought down the handset on the cradle. The handset did not sit right and slipped here and there under his grip. He lifted it slightly and tossed it into the cradle with a bang.

'Yes?' he asked both Haleema and the man, swinging his head from her to him to her once again. His voice was spooky and ghostly, like a stereo running on low voltage.

Haleema re-narrated the brief version.

The producer began to look uncomfortable even before she finished.

'Radio doesn't air this kind of news,' he said stiffly. 'Look for a newspaper instead.'

'Behind the radio station is the TV station,' the bearded man apprised Haleema while showing her out. 'You can try there, maybe they will…' he said.

At the TV station, Haleema crossed a long, winding cement path that ran through the middle of a large compound before stopping at some detached huts that looked like small wooden barracks. The doors of all the huts were closed shut. She gently knocked at the door of the first one, and it went ajar. The room was warm and almost dark. Haleema hesitantly explored it. There were some empty wooden chairs around a coal *bukhari* whose embers seemed to have died out long ago. There was a large table beside the chairs littered with groundnut shells and crumpled paper. At once a muffled voice called from somewhere further inside. 'Who is it?'

A keener glance, after she had adjusted her eyes to the darkness of the room, and Haleema found there was a closet on the other side of the room. She advanced forward and found a bleak entrance to a small area on the right. The partitioned wall was made of plywood. There, further inside, she saw a young woman sitting before a large mirror. Under the mirror there was a crude wooden counter full of tweezers, lipsticks, rouges, foundations, combs, cotton, scissors and cheap cosmetics. The woman was trying to fix a bunch of false eyelashes on her right eyelid. She was already done with the left one. When she saw Haleema in the mirror she suspended her forefinger midway, with the eyelashes on its tip, in the air. She spoke to Haleema's reflection.

'Yes, what do you want?' she asked.

'I am looking for someone who could give my news,' Haleema said in a hesitant, uncertain voice.

'What news?'

Haleema quickly narrated the brief version.

'I can take you to the news producer but I am sure meeting him will be futile. He will tell you, as he always calls this kind of stuff, that it is "dangerous and unconventional". Anyway, go out, turn right and you'll see a large grey building with white windows. Ground floor, Room 24,' the woman said, attaching the eyelashes to her eye. She blinked her eyes exactly thrice to test if the lashes had fixed properly.

Haleema came out and vapidly gazed at the said building, reluctantly walking some paces towards it, before stopping and turning to leave. She considered the young woman's advice and left.

On the bus back home, she sat behind a man who was reading an Urdu newspaper. *Newspaper*! She disembarked on Residency Road near a wooden pushcart selling unshelled water nuts and popcorn in front of the long-shut, desolated Regal Cinema, now an army camp too. She asked the cart owner for directions to the Press Enclave where the offices of various Urdu and English newspapers were. He pointed to his left. 'There. First left.' She was not sure where to go in Press Enclave. She saw a boy with a camera slung over his neck standing at a makeshift tea stall. He was carefully taking quick sips from a dirty cup with multiple hairline cracks and swiftly nibbling at the already bitten edge of a sugar-kissed rectangular *bakirkhaani*.

'Could you tell me where BBC is?' Haleema asked, as BBC was the only name she could think of.

The boy, still munching, gestured with the hand that held his tea towards the other direction.

The BBC's Srinagar bureau was dreaded by visitors. A month ago, their photographer had died when a parcel-bomb had exploded in the reception of its outhouse office. Izhar had seen pieces of Mushtaq stuck to its walls. Mushtaq's torn face had lain like a prosthetic mask near his head.

Since then, officially, the BBC cottage in Press Enclave was just a masquerade. Izhar operated from unknown places now.

When Haleema knocked, a tubby man opened it and cocked his head out. He asked Haleema who she was and what she wanted. Haleema gave her introduction. The tubby man asked her to wait. He left the door ajar, went inside, into what looked like a little alley, dialled a number and spoke short Kashmiri sentences in a low voice into the phone. Then he hung up and ushered Haleema into a small room with a frowsty smell. The tubby man asked her to wait there. He watched her silently for some time and then initiated a conversation. He told her about the blast. He told her that she was sitting in the same room where it had occurred. He talked and talked, without even asking Haleema to speak or respond.

Haleema looked around. The dark green paint on the walls looked fresh. She tried to imagine the blast in her mind.

The windows of the small room were new and densely grilled. Along with a thick wooden door, the entrance now had one of iron too. All the windows and doors were painted white. The entry to the residential office was through the outhouse. Between the outhouse and the office was a narrow lawn.

A wooden shelf sat in the corner of the room, stacked with dusty newspapers. A shiny black helmet sat on the upper shelf, with a sticker that read 'Billboard' pasted on it. A muffler hung by the window's bolt, its woollen tassels drooping perfectly. Haleema padded her elbow with the armrest and cupped her jaw in her fingers. And waited.

About half an hour later, Izhar walked in.

'*Assalaam-u-Alaiqum*,' he said. He wore grey pants and a shiny black leather jacket. There was a roll of newspapers sticking under his arm. He threw the roll on a chair and sat across Haleema. 'Sorry, I was busy with a report. It took some time. You don't know me but I know you very well,' he said, a hint of smile in his eyes.

Haleema was pleasantly surprised.

'I was there when your father…' Izhar said, panning his eyes to the floor. 'I was there all day. I did the story for BBC.'

'May God keep you in good health. I wouldn't know anything. That day was like doomsday for me. That day was a Karbala. That day…' Haleema said.

'I can understand how difficult it must have been,' he said, 'I can imagine, I was there. I was witness to it.'

'Dear, something more tragic has happened since Ab Jaan's death, and it has not given me even the time to mourn him properly. Something more painful…' Haleema sighed.

Izhar furrowed his brow and leaned forward in his chair. 'What?' he asked with utter curiosity. 'What happened?'

Haleema narrated the full version.

A long silence fell in the room once she was done.

'You should have come to me straight,' Izhar said. He leaned back and put his right ankle over his left knee. 'But how would one know!' he said, looking down at the floor. 'How would one know?'

He promised her a small report on the BBC. 'And let me accompany you to some local newspapers as well. Someone will carry the news,' he said.

Izhar took her across Press Enclave towards the office of the Urdu newspaper *Waadi ki Aawaz*. The paper's office was on the top floor of a tall building. Izhar shook a green net-door by its handle. A figure approached the door, his silhouette falling across the net. The boy worked as a stringer for the paper and recognized Izhar immediately, greeting him respectfully with a smile, and unbolted the door.

'Is Shaida sahib there?' Izhar asked him.

'Yes sir,' the boy replied and guided them towards the editor's chambers.

Izhar opened the door to his office and said salaam. Shaida immediately rose from his chair and hugged him at length.

G.N. Shaida's office was dimly lit. He sat behind a large table. His thick horn-rimmed glasses sat on a pile of papers on the table next to his neatly folded prayer rug. His office overlooked Pratab Park. Haleema looked out through the window. It was the first time she had seen the park from such a height. Despite being torn between tragedy and misery, she still couldn't help looking at the park and its surroundings. She noticed the parched cement pool in the centre of the park, with garbage littering its dry bottom. Its fountains were dry too. The paint on the big cement umbrellas along the pool had begun to peel as well. Next to the locked gate, a trooper was wearily jerking his knees inside out. Suddenly Haleema became aware of her presence in Shaida's office. Izhar narrated Haleema's full version to Shaida.

'You know, Izhar, the government has already stopped advertising with us because we publish this human rights stuff. They have been accusing us of sensationalism. Ha! Ha! They say that we do not follow their policy. But I don't care,' Shaida said, 'Haleema's grief will still be printed in my paper.' He pressed the steel bell on his table. Then he twisted the bell with both hands to wind it up for his next call and put it back. The boy appeared. 'Call Irshad,' Shaida ordered him.

'It will be on the front page in tomorrow's edition,' Shaida told Haleema.

Thanking Shaida, Izhar and Haleema walked off. 'Don't hesitate to get in touch if there is anything I can do,' Izhar told Haleema.

'You are a wonderful man, dearest brother,' she said.

'I suggest you do something more, something very important – approach the court,' Izhar said and paused, 'otherwise they will play with you. You will be tossed around like a shuttlecock.'

'I don't know how. I have never been to a court,' she said.

'I shall accompany you to a lawyer friend of mine. He is a member of the bar. He can take your case.'

'How much would he charge me for that?' Haleema asked innocently.

Izhar smiled. 'Nothing. He will not charge you for something like this.'

'May God keep you,' Haleema said gratefully.

Haleema couldn't sleep that night, eagerly waiting for the dawn. Sleepless, she went out and sat on the verandah. The icy winds bit into her. The leaves on the trees had drooped and were gently swishing in the windy chill. In the distance, a faint sound of gunshots and barking dogs emerged. Then a louder drone of an automatic's burst. Then a thunderbolt from a grenade. From somewhere, a rumble of gunfire tore the air.

She was indifferent now to the sounds of war. The strewn leaves on the path scraped against it when a slow breeze swept them away. A cat jumped down from a wall onto the path, purred and passed on. Haleema stood on the verandah, listening to the new sounds of the night, the new music of Kashmir.

At dawn, the sky had a milky overcast. The wooden gate had jammed with crusted rime. Haleema loitered out to the road and waited for the newspaper hawker. Troops patrolling the road passed her. They were going from bunker to bunker, delivering breakfasts to their fellow men. Monkey-capped, they slouched with the steel tiffins, flasks, canes and giant searchlights in their hands.

The two troopers who led the party at the front and two more at the back wore bulletproof vests. They were probing roadside garbage, underground pipes and culverts with hooked iron rods and mine detectors.

They stared at Haleema but said nothing.

A mufflered boy passed by. He rode a bicycle loaded with newspapers on its carrier and in a basket up front. He wore a feather jacket under his *pheran* that made him look fat. Haleema stopped him and asked for a copy of *Waadi ki Aawaz*. He stopped, straddling the rod of his bicycle, then turned his body sideways and reached for a bundle on the carrier. He wet his bare fingertips on his tongue and picked out a copy.

Haleema gave him a fiver. He shook the side-pocket of his *pheran*. The coins in it tinkled. He expertly took out four one-rupee coins without looking at them.

Haleema began looking for the news about Imran. As usual, the lead story carried a picture of the dead under the headline: *Sheher mein Mazeed Paanch Afraad Halaak* – 'Five More Dead in the City'.

She scanned the first page while simultaneously walking and tripping on the pebbles. And there it was, at the bottom of the page. A small photo of Imran, in black-and-white, was printed with the story. She kissed it, her eyes moist. The photo was surrounded by the news of his disappearance in Urdu (in brief version). She rolled the newspaper and strutted briskly towards the house.

She sat in the kitchen, spread the paper out and read the news aloud. The headline said, *Haleema ka Dugna Sadma* – 'Haleema's Double Tragedy'. A portion of the news continued on the third page. She flipped to the page and searched for the remainder among pictures of masked insurgents consoling haggard relatives of their deceased companions with a copy of the Quran. She continued to read the report, erring with some long and twisted words she was unfamiliar with. She read the report several times. And when she was satisfied, she folded the newspaper carefully and tucked it into the heirloom tin trunk.

9

Papa 2

Outside the SSP's office, Haleema raved and wept bitterly. She had been waiting to meet him for two hours before she lost her patience and snatched a guard's rifle in frustration. She pointed the barrel at her chest and threw its butt into the guard's hands. 'Kill me!' she shrieked in utter frustration. The guard looked on vacantly. 'Come on, shoot me! I don't want to live!'

The guard jerkily pulled back the gun and seized it firmly in his hands.

He ushered her into the SSP's office.

'You have been playing with me for the last month. Why won't you tell me where my son is?' Haleema screamed at the SSP, who was surprised at this sudden intrusion into his space.

'Calm down. Calm down. Drink some water,' the SSP pacified her. 'I have enquired to the best of my efforts. My sources say a young boy has been admitted to the army hospital. Maybe he is your son. I will arrange a pass for you from the IG's office and send you to the hospital. My driver will accompany you. Is that okay?' the SSP asked.

'*Khudaay thavinai muujood*, may God keep you,' Haleema said, smiling through her tears. 'Please do something, please please please,' she said gratefully.

'Come tomorrow.'

On her way to the army hospital, armed with a pink-coloured gate pass, she asked the SSP's driver to stop for a minute at a shrine. She tore a strip off the edge of her dupatta, tied it to the grille of the shrine and made a wish. *The knot will be untied when I will have found him, perhaps.*

The army hospital was behind the Badami Bagh Cantonment. Its windows were covered with olive-green army blankets. Inside, captive young boys and men recovered from custodial torture, only to become fit again for further interrogations and torture.

Haleema saw limbless, fingerless, nailless, hairless, toothless, eyeless, earless detainees – a variety of wriggling, howling, yowling amputated souls. A cold flux ran down her spine. The scene dazed her.

'I don't think they can walk now, even with prosthetics,' the SSP's driver whispered furtively into Haleema's ear. She didn't respond.

She surveyed the boys whose kidneys had failed. They had been trampled over by cement rollers. All were handcuffed to their iron beds. The rusty, cold chains were clanking against the metal frames. *Has Imran gone through the same treatment*? She thought for a second, and then shook it off. *God forbid.*

She saw a handsome young man who was on a ventilator; they learnt his anus had been bleeding uncontrollably.

'A rod through his gut, I bet,' the driver whispered.

She checked all the wards bed by bed. There was no trace of Imran. She tried to ask some boys about Imran, describing him, but no one had a clue. The subedar in charge denied having hospitalized Imran or any boy resembling him. When he saw Haleema and the driver taking notes of the admitted keenly, he ordered them to leave immediately. 'Hurry up,' he said.

She lost count of the days that slipped by. Time had stopped for her and she now waited for it to unfreeze itself. With Imran's disappearance, the painful memory of Ab Jaan's death had begun to diminish. One torment eased her out of the other. It seemed as if Ab Jaan had been killed many decades ago.

One sunny morning in May, she approached member of Parliament Rafi Bhat to try her luck. Seed-tufts from the poplars were dropping to the ground like a cotton blizzard. It was the most difficult month for Haleema's lungs, the beginning of summer. The air was fresh yet fraught with pollen dust and poplar seeds.

A polished piece of black marble on a pillar beside the large iron gate outside Rafi Bhat's palatial house announced the residence as Bhat Manzil. Bhat expected dozens of people, mostly burqa-cloaked women, knocking at his door for help every morning. Especially mothers whose boys were picked up. He was familiar with such cases and dealt with them in a mechanical way. It was routine to consider the grievance, show immense sympathy and count each help-seeker as a future voter. All his politician friends and rivals had already left the valley and now sought refuge in Jammu or New Delhi, but he had stayed back.

Haleema sat on Bhat's verandah and gazed at the crewel curtains veiling the enormous glass windows of his drawing room. Visitors were supposed to wait there until he appeared to listen to their grievances. So she waited, observing his neatly mowed lawn, all green and without a speck of poplar seeds, and the pruned larches, firs and spruces surrounding the greenery. A little pigeon house sat on a marble pedestal in a corner. The hedges fencing the garden had been shaped into a pattern of troughs and crests.

For a brief moment Haleema thought she was dreaming. It was after a long time she had seen a green piece of earth like this garden. *A garden, incredibly incompatible to the Kashmir outside this house.* Her thoughts strayed to her untrimmed, unpruned patch of a lawn, a spectacle of despair and loss. She thought of the weeds that had grown everywhere. Flowerbeds that once smiled from their clumps of foxgloves, mimosas, pansies and carnations had vanished under tufts of overgrown grass. The unshorn poplars had begun to block the sun, causing the garden to bald. There were now patches where the earth was naked. Heaps of fallen leaves from last autumn still rotted there.

The orchard too had had its share of decline. Most of its trees were now afflicted with plum-pox, with yellow blotches on the leaves and deformed fruit. The local children would pilfer the rest of the fruit that the disease spared. It was Ab Jaan who would get the trees sprayed at the right intervals of the fruiting season. It was he who would get the earth loosened around the roots, weeding the space between the trees.

Their kitchen garden had disappeared in the dense clumps of brambles and wild thickets of unknown shrubbery and weeds. The ridges that divided the beds had begun to wear down and flatten. The soil had fused back to a hard texture. Clover, dandelions, wild daisy, turf grass, moss, sparse clusters of nettle and poppy: nature had crept back in, and slowly started reclaiming everything.

Haleema sat quietly, helplessly marvelling at Bhat's neatly maintained garden, and quickly decided that she would not allow his lawn to be part of her memory. She looked over to a white iron swing at one end of the lawn and imagined it rocking.

Behind the swing was a small swimming pool with icy blue water, where no one swam. Rafi lived alone in his large house. His children were in the US, studying medicine or engineering. His wife had eloped with a political rival, but in public he said he had divorced her, something people pretended to agree with.

Clean-shaven, Rafi Bhat appeared, donning a splendidly embroidered rat-grey tweed gown with a long cigarette between his lips.

'What did you say your name was?' he asked her, not sitting down.

'Haleema, *haz*,' Haleema said.

'*Vary* good. *Vary* good,' he coughed and sat on a couch. 'So what is the story?' he asked.

Haleema narrated the full version. She told it sequentially, bit by bit, not missing a single fact or detail. And he kept responding with 'Vary good', appreciating the steps Haleema had already taken to trace Imran. When she finished, he took a while to respond.

'I will look into the matter. Don't worry,' he said, coughing and cursing the poplars even when there was no trace of the seed on his premises, which was always kept clean by his three servants. Haleema left Bhat Manzil with a hope.

In the following months she continued to make rounds of Bhat's house. Then one day he asked her, 'Have you ever thought about yourself?' He took a long drag from his cigarette. 'You are wasting your beauty and time in vain.' With his forefinger, he tapped the ash into the empty cup of tea he had just drunk out of. 'Don't you think if we two meet, we can find him in a day? Just think...Well, I assure you your son will be with you tomorrow, but meanwhile, give it a good thought. Hmm?' He chuckled. 'Expect the army to drop him at your nearest police station on 15th August. I have sent a message across, to all senior officers. They have assured me that they will locate your son and possibly deliver him at your concerned police station on Independence Day.'

The tone of his assurance was so convincing that Haleema carelessly rejected the idea of slapping him for his suggestive proposal.

On 15 August, for the sake of relative mercy, the army had promised to release boys pressed on venial charges. It was an 'Independence Day Gift', the army said in its presser to the media.

To unfurl the Indian tricolour, the whole valley was put under curfew. The army sieged the schools and stadiums days before to prevent them from insurgent attacks or protests. All immediate societies that surrounded these places were sanitized and occupied in advance. The army posted makeshift pickets and posted snipers on rooftops and verandahs of houses to keep a vigil on any subversion.

Kashmiris marked the day as a 'Black Day', and observed blackouts at night. Early that morning, Haleema made *tahri* – rice sautéed in turmeric, shallots and salt – for thanksgiving to the local people. At the prospect of Imran's release, she spread a double-mattress in a corner of the drawing room where he was supposed to sit for the visitors. Then she went to the Saddar Police Station where the army was expected to hand Imran over.

The police told Haleema they did not know about any handover from any battalion. But Haleema continued to wait. Hours passed and no one arrived.

'See, they are just misleading you. Looking for your son this way will result in nothing and will keep you waiting forever,' the SHO at the station sympathized with Haleema.

Haleema didn't reply.

'The army takes most of their catches to Papa 2 Interrogation Centre,' the SHO said.

'*Papa 2*? Yes, I have been hearing its name,' Haleema said.

'Yes. They have two main interrogation centres in Srinagar: Papa 1 and Papa 2. Most of their detainees go to Papa 2, at Gupkar Road. You must visit it. Maybe you will find him or at least get a clue there.'

'God-willing. Maybe,' Haleema said in a defeated voice.

She returned glum from the police station at night.

On *arfa*, a day before Eid, while people cooked their ceremonial dishes – *rista* (pounded meatballs), kebabs and *yakhni* – for the Eid lunch, Haleema sat counting the cross-marked days on her calendar until it prickled her legs and made her back sore and her body numb.

That whole night she listened to her sometimes-fast-sometimes-slow pulse from her head under the pillow. To pass the time, she counted it. She lost the count and gave up. Then, with every tick and tock of the clock, she counted the time. Seconds. Minutes. Hours.

She had grown habitually insomniac now. Dark brown patches had developed under her eyes. Incipient wrinkles criss-crossed her face, while her cheeks had begun to sag.

The following morning, Haleema hired an auto-rickshaw from the stand near the shrine. The air was filled with cotton seed-tufts. All along the way, she tried to count the bunkers, checkpoints and army camps, whose numbers had insidiously grown since everything began. Kashmir almost couldn't tell itself from the maze of bunkers. Yet, she lost count of them too.

On Amira Kadal, the auto-rickshaw hurtled clumsily through traffic. Haleema spotted the half-gutted buildings and shops that had been set on fire a year ago by the army while reprimanding another insurgent attack down the bridge. Slogans of Azaadi had been stencilled on every second wall in the city in green. Pigeons sat on power lines like beads on a thread.

Lal Chowk wore an alien look. The market was almost closed. Footpaths were occupied by beggars and strangers. Bleating sacrificial sheep and goats looked on from everywhere, while kids pulled their parents to buy toys sold from cots. Haleema desperately looked left and right, surveying here and there, hoping by chance she would find him walking down a footpath. *What if I spot his face in the crowd?* A boy with as thin a haircut as Imran, with the same height and stance, walked across her. *Let me turn around and see...oh*! It was not him; just a mere pedestrian walking at Dalgate.

On Boulevard Road, the auto-rickshaw sped up. The waters of the Dal and the breeze from it calmed her. Here too, at every ten paces along the shore, stood a trooper with his finger on the trigger.

The Dal brought back the memory of a family picnic, when Ab Jaan had taken Haleema and Imran for a *shikara* ride. She even remembered the ice cream Imran had wanted to have at Char Chinaari: the orange ice-candy that turned his tongue orange. Imran had let his fingers bruise the surface of the sparkling Dal as the *shikara* cruised, and then thrown water on her initiating a water fight.

A splash of water on her face brought Haleema back. The auto-rickshaw stopped past Hotel Welcome, before the last turn, to give way to a passing convoy of dozens of army trucks. Each truck had a trooper – masked in a black scarf and wearing black goggles –

popping out from under the turreted roof with a heavy ordnance machine gun. The convoy was escorted by two armoured jeeps whose jammer-aerials waggled behind them.

Named after a wireless language code, Papa 2 concealed the purpose of a place that was a paradox: it was beautiful, and horrible, at the same time.

Beautiful, because it overlooked Dal Lake and its houseboats and *shikaras* from the foothills of Mount Harmukh. Further, in the nebulous, snow-draped mountains to the north of Ganderbal, was where the hillock where Maqhdoom Sahib's shrine lay.

Horrible, because it was once the stately mansion of the last monarch of Kashmir that had now been transformed into a torture centre.

The entire sylvan landscape was garrisoned.

Haleema alighted at the base of a sloped road that led towards the Grand Palace, and trekked up to Papa 2 punctuated by long restive, breathy intervals. At each interval she pumped her inhaler twice. She joined a long queue of parents, siblings and kin at the high, spiky iron gate of Papa 2. The gate was flanked by two watch posts. Relatives carried bags full of ironed clothes, clean underwear, toothpaste, soaps, shaving kits, flip-flops, handkerchiefs, medicines, radio sets, fruits, food, and cartons of glucose.

The guards frisked everybody's belongings. They stirred the chicken soup and stoked the rice in the tiffin boxes with tablespoons. They kneaded the clothes, shook the eggs, and squeezed the tubes of toothpaste, squiggling out some paste as sample. Shaving kits, radio sets, letters and money were not allowed. The relatives ambled inside Papa 2, where they were asked to wait.

'Where are you going?' the guard asked Haleema, army rigour in his voice, when she tried to follow the others.

'To see if my son is there. Major Aman Kushwaha picked him up.'

'"*To see if my son is there*?" What are you saying? Do you have any pass or confirmation or have you come here for the first time?'

'I don't know where he is. I want to see if he is here. This is the first time I have come here, as it is Eid today.' Haleema loathed everything about the trooper.

'We cannot allow visits like this. Unless you have a confirmation.'

'Please, brother. I just want to see for myself.'

The guard gently pushed her out. She was reluctant.

'It is not possible. See, we are releasing some boys today because of Eid. Stay out and sit there,' the guard pointed towards a poplar across the road, 'and then see if he is among them.'

She sat under the tree, hugging her knees and gazing at the gate. She could only see a barrack on a raised mound of earth from where she was sitting. Her hand began fumbling with her surroundings and aimlessly cutting the blades of grass. She gazed at the seed-tufts floating against the background of Papa 2 and the Zabarwan hills behind it. Nearby was a creeper whose yellow flowers had stamens that tasted like *kahwa*. Imran was fond of the flower.

Minutes later, she saw a file of blindfolded boys being led down a flight of stairs to the invisible premises of Papa 2. Then for a long time there was no movement. No one appeared at the gate.

Hours passed; she waited and wriggled. Her mouth had dried up. She was feeling thirsty, hungry and suicidal. Yet each time she thought of death, she felt strictly accountable to life. It was the hope of seeing Imran that made her feel so. She saw crows and vultures hovering on the horizon over the ridges of Zabarwan. Endless coils of barbed wire topped the high walls around Papa 2. She watched army convoys pass in and out of the camp. Troopers looked curiously at her as they passed but said nothing.

In the late afternoon, a few boys walked out with their relatives. Some of them limped and some had to be supported to walk. An old rustic-looking woman lifted her sick son and mounted him onto her back. The woman's hair was grizzled over her temples. She was shorter and slimmer than Haleema but tougher and more audacious.

When all the relatives came out, Haleema stood up. She was tired of sitting. She felt as if all her bones were going to break on their own. She walked towards the gate.

'Why are you still here?' the guard asked strictly.

'He is not among them. I want to check inside. I have been waiting for so long. Have mercy on me.'

'I told you, it is not permitted. Go away.'

'He is my only son. Let me see for myself. Let me ask the officer inside,' Haleema said desperately, crying.

'You won't understand. I said go home.'

'I won't, until I see him,' she said a bit stiffly.

'Then wait here till the next Eid.'

The guard went inside and shut the gate in her face.

10

Valley Hiardressers

Haleema briskly walked down the slope of Papa 2 towards Boulevard Road, following the released boys and their relatives. They had nearly scuttled away, except for Jana, the seemingly fragile yet energetic old woman whose son Rehbar was mounted on her back.

At the turnoff on Boulevard Road, Jana unmounted him and sat him against a downed shutter of a handicraft emporium. She squatted close to the edge of the road, waiting for an empty rickshaw to pass, and kept stealing quick glances at Rehbar. He looked pale and unwashed; his hair was dishevelled and matted. He wore a sleeveless home-knitted coffee-brown sweater, with a pattern of cubes. Huffing, Haleema reached there.

Helmeted bikers and occupied rickshaws whizzed by, both outnumbered by army convoys.

'Did you meet any boy inside Papa 2 called Imran?' Haleema asked Rehbar, describing Imran in great detail.

'Yes. There was a boy called that, very young, of your description. But not at Papa 2. I saw him at Badami Bagh Cantonment. Not here. And not now, but before I was shifted to Papa 2.'

'*Really? What was he saying? How is he? Where is he now?*' Haleema was breathless. A smile tugged at the creases near the corners of her eyes. This was the first time she had come across a clue, an inkling of Imran's presence. She wiped off a tear that had begun to stream down her cheek.

'He said he was from Natipora...' Rehbar said. Jana looked intently at Haleema. She seemed pleased that her son knew about a boy whose mother was looking for him.

'Yes, and?' Haleema asked excitedly. Her hands trembled.

'And that he had nobody at home except his mother…'

'*Lag'ya balay'i*!' Haleema interrupted Rehbar, wishing she were there to shield Imran from harm.

'…he said his mother was alone and whom he was sulking with because she had not come to take him home,' Rehbar continued in an exhausted voice, sounding sick.

'And?' Haleema snivelled.

'He would not eat and drink. He would sit in a corner of the eight-by-eight cell for hours, burying his head between his knees till the guards would come and bark at him or twiddle his ear or smack him or make him do sit-ups.'

'How do I get there?' Haleema asked impatiently.

'It is impossible to go there. The barrack is at the rear of the cantonment and it has been a long time since I was shifted to Papa 2. They will not allow anyone to visit the cantonment. Even if you have the governor's pass, they won't.'

'So? What should I do?'

'...there was a barber, Abdus Salaam. Only he was allowed to go in. He came to shave the detainees every fortnight. He was from Pampore. He shaved your son's head once too.'

'Really?'

'I don't know exactly where in Pampore but he once said his shop was very close to the cantonment. The army would not go to Srinagar looking for a barber.'

'Right.'

Jana did not interrupt while Haleema quizzed Rehbar but smiled at her own strange satisfaction that her son could at least inform another dismayed woman about her son's whereabouts. Rehbar's releasing order fluttered in her hand. It was but half a leaf of thin white paper, stained with typewritten lines and affixed with the seal and signature of the subedar underneath, but it counted for a lot. It read:

RELEASING ORDER

After acquiring an undertaking from his mother Jana Akhtar that he will not indulge in militancy again, Rehbar Khan, S/o: Rahim Khan, R/o: Dardpora, Kupwara, is being released on the occasion of Eid, 21 May. He will not be unnecessarily detained again without any solid grounds of his involvement in militancy.

Jana carefully folded the paper and tucked it in the side-pocket of her ragged, paisley-printed *pheran*. She ran her hand down to the depths of the pocket to ensure that the paper settled in its bottom. Finally, an empty rickshaw passed by. She hawked it down and helped her son get into the back seat.

'Where are you going?' Haleema asked her.

'As of now, to Soura hospital. He doesn't look too well,' Jana replied.

'Yes, you must. And could you drop me at Dalgate?' Haleema queried. 'If it's not a bother.'

'Please.'

'You cannot go all the way to Kupwara if you need something when you are at the hospital. Please feel free to come to my place in Natipora,' Haleema offered. The wind from Dal Lake drowned out their voices so she had to shout out her address to them.

Haleema disembarked at Dalgate and boarded a lazily taxiing bus to Batwara, where the cantonment was. The butt-beaten black leather seats in the bus were vacant. The bus conductor continued to holler outside, emphatically telling all potential passengers the bus was about to leave.

The bus snailed over some distance after it finally began to move. Only when half the seats were filled – mostly children in fancy Eid dresses and yellow-rimmed toy goggles, carrying toy guns or funky clutches – did it pick up speed.

Haleema got down at Sonwar and looked for barbers on both sides of the road. She passed a row of pushcarts that sold toys and *seemni*, *khandd-gaaziri* and *basrakh*, all special Eid snacks. She ambled past huddled-up men gossiping on shop sills, past a line of closed shops and a silent, dusky, self-absorbed man who sold bamboo flutes and duck-shaped balloons, incessantly chafing over them to issue a rough screech, chrrr, to attract customers, mostly children.

The sun was about to set and bright daylight was soon turning into a shade of honey. She stopped at an inconspicuous barbershop diagonally across the cantonment's gate. An elaborate sign over the shop read: 'Valley Hiardressers', with the word 'Hair' misspelt. A pair of scissors and a comb crisscrossing each other had been painted between the two words. Haleema hesitantly entered the shop.

A few men awaited their turns. The salon was filled with their collective silence and the only sound that could be heard was the click-click of the scissors and the occasional tap of the comb. One customer was reading an outdated magazine, held upright in front of his eyes, the back cover featuring an advertisement of two dolphins jumping out of an icy blue ocean.

All the eyes in the shop turned to Haleema as she entered. For a moment she was confused, unsure about what to do next.

Two men, one older and the other younger – clearly an apprentice – were snipping about the steady heads of two customers seated calmly on tall chairs, facing a large mirror. There was another mirror opposite the large one that reflected the scruffs. Cut tresses of hair littered the floor like dead leeches. Haleema noticed the mirrors endlessly reflected each other – mirror within a mirror within another mirror… For a fraction of a moment she wondered about the eternity of mirrors. She had never seen any such thing, a common enough occurrence at a barbershop. She quickly shook herself out of it. Besides the scissors, combs, tubes of shaving cream, shaving brushes and other requisite objects on the sunmica counter, she noted a plastic bottle of Jasmine talcum powder. It reminded her of Imran's childhood. She kept staring at the bottle until the older man spoke to her.

'Yes, *humsheera*. How can I help you, sister?'

'What is your good name?' Haleema asked him.

'Gulzar Ahmad. Why?'

'I have come a long way looking for Abdus Salaam of Pampore. I thought you would be him.'

'Yes, Salaam *wasta* does work here, but he is off today because of Eid. Could I be of any assistance?' He began sharpening his blade, first on a strop and then on a whetstone that sat on a chipping countertop.

'Thank you, but I want to see Salaam sahib,' Haleema urged. 'It is very urgent.'

'Okay. I will give you the directions to his house... Get down at Kadalabal bus stop. Take the first right – it's a wide lane with a giant chinar – walk straight until you see a flour mill. Turn right at the flour mill, then the first right again; it's the last house on the right, with a black gate.'

'Many thanks, brother. Many thanks.'

Haleema flagged down a rickshaw and passed through a long garrisoned road towards Pantha Chowk. Two armed troops stopped the rickshaw at the Pantha Chowk crossing. One of them popped his head inside and asked for the driver's identity card. 'Do you have the *atenty* card with you?' Haleema asked him.

'I don't have all the papers but how can one forget the identity card? Don't worry, I have it,' he said with a cold, suppressed smile. 'Here,' he told the trooper, carefully garnering a laminated card out of a bundle of worn paper chits and oddly folded banknotes from his shirt pocket.

The trooper compared the photo with the driver's face. He returned it to him without reading the other particulars, satisfied by the photograph. He then turned to Haleema. 'Where to?'

'*Mera beta dhoondtay hain. Aap log hi pakad ke ley gaye.* I am looking for my son, who was picked up by you folks only,' she replied in broken Urdu.

The trooper got confused and looked at his mate on the other side of the auto. The mate blinked back at him. They gestured at the driver to leave.

Haleema began to tell her story to the auto driver.

In a way, it was now a strange, a different kind of psychological torture to be compelled to tell her story to anyone from the beginning, in proper order, without missing a single detail, till the end. With time she had begun to forget details. She would remember them later, after finishing the narration, and would remind her listener of the details she had missed. The only thing she couldn't recall was how many, how many people exactly, had she narrated the story to.

The auto driver dropped her at the crumbling Kadalabal bus stop. She took out her small maroon purse to pay the fare. The seams of the purse had frayed, along its defunct zip. The driver noticed it while she picked through a few ragged tenners, folded and creased in fourths. Without looking at her, he bent to his left and started his auto. He gave the accelerator a few back-and-forths and told her, 'Keep the money. I can't take money from you,' and left.

Haleema called him back loudly but he ignored her. She stuffed the money back into her purse. '*Raechh kaernai, miyon Khuadaai,* may God protect you,' she prayed under her breath.

Abdus Salaam lived in an unpainted, unplastered three-storeyed wood-and-brick house. Only the compound wall was made of concrete. Three earthen vases of cacti sat equidistant from each other over the cement pylon frame of the black gate. The gate was ajar, and the lawn reeked of cow dung. A child sat on the verandah, playing with a steel spoon, its snot running down to its lips. Each time the child pulled back the snot it bubbled at his nostrils.

A metre away from the child, a goat sat on a flattened gunnysack, tethered to a pillar on the verandah, bleating incessantly. A burst of black pellets was scattered near its tail.

When Haleema tapped hard on the backside of the gate, a hoary man with stubbled and caved-in cheeks walked out and stood in the doorway. He was chewing on something. 'Yes? Who are you looking for?' he asked, chewing and rolling whatever was in his mouth.

'Can I sit first?' said Haleema, gathering her breath.

'*Ahan haz*, sure you can.'

He unrolled a reed mat and sat her on the cleaner side of the verandah. '*Nahidai*!' he hollered in the direction of the doorway, 'take Wasim inside.'

A young girl in a parrot-green shalwar-kameez emerged from the doorway.

'My daughter,' the man quickly introduced the girl to Haleema. The girl looked at her curiously.

'So, what is it?' the man asked Haleema.

'You would be Abdus Salaam?' Haleema confirmed.

'Indeed, I am Abdus Salaam.'

'Okay. Here…' Haleema showed him a picture of Imran and told him the story.

'Hmm!' Abdus Salaam sighed after listening patiently. After a long pause, he spoke: 'Since my shop was very close to the cantonment, the army called me in once. A major wanted a shave. Perhaps their barber was not available. But it so happened that they called me once more; I had to give a haircut and shoulder massage to a subedar. It became a sort of a routine after that. They began to call me more often. They would come looking for me, and ask my apprentices when I wasn't at the shop. Gradually they introduced me to their detainees. At the back of the cantonment is a building called Butcher House, where the boys were detained and interrogated.

'Two months ago I saw a boy who resembles the picture you have. I saw him last when he refused to get a shave.'

'What was his condition? I mean, was he all right?' Haleema asked, now breathless.

'He seemed to be physically all right. But he was too scared. Numb. He didn't talk much.'

'What was he wearing? Did he have enough clothes?'

'A long oversized trench coat. I don't know what he was wearing inside it.'

'After a fortnight,' continued Abdus Salaam, 'I saw a new lot of kids. The guard told me the previous detainees had been shifted to some other place, which he did not know. This new lot was horrible to look at. They had been tortured recently. I couldn't even shave them properly as the skin fell off their faces. "They pulled it out with pliers," one of them told me with great difficulty.

'It was hair-raising. Some of them requested me to feed them the hot water I had washed my shaving brush with. They had been as thirsty as a desert. One's forearms had turned septic. I tried rubbing alum over it. But the infection wouldn't go so easily.'

Haleema sighed and listened keenly.

'Haunting stories. Someday I shall tell them to everyone... The guards began to suspect that I might tell others what I saw inside the cells. One day, the subedar paid me for the previous two fortnights; they had begun paying me on a monthly basis. "We won't need you now. Our barber has returned," he told me.

'I have been struggling with the memories since then. But I am not supposed to tell you these things. As far as your son is concerned, by the standards in those cells, he was fine when I last saw him. Only God knows...'

Haleema wiped her tears.

Abdus Salaam's daughter brought out an earless, bowl-like cup and *bakirkhanis* along with a white thermos of *nuun chai* on a steel tray. A few drops of the tea had spilled around the cup.

'There was no need for this. In fact, I am sorry I disturbed you on Eid. Terribly sorry,' Haleema apologized.

As the girl began to pour the tea into a cup, the thermos's lid fell off amid the tea's gurgles.

'*Haai*! I am sorry,' the girl said nervously, putting the lid back and screwing it close. Haleema noticed bits of tea and cream sticking to the rotting rubber washer of the lid.

'It is only a cup of tea, and since today is Eid… How can we let you go without a cup of tea at least? Please,' Abdus Salaam beckoned Haleema towards the cup.

They didn't speak as Haleema drank the tea. The girl brought out the child once again, sat it in the lap of Abdus Salaam and went back inside. Haleema could now see it was a boy. He continued to play with the same spoon, licking and waving it in the air, babbling. He already resembled Salaam's daughter. The boy wore new plain white kurta-pyjamas that already had food stains all over it. The snot had begun to dry under his nose.

Haleema blew on the tea and took small sips, studying the child intently.

'My grandson… His name is Wasim. Please have some *bakirkhani*…you are only drinking the tea… Please break a crisp *bakirkhani* into the cup,' Salaam insisted.

Salaam's daughter came out again and went straight to Haleema, sat down and broke a *bakirkhani* into her cup.

'Umm! Not much…it upsets my stomach,' Haleema resisted politely.

The girl ignored her courteously. 'It is only a little,' she said with a stiff smile, dropping the last few crumbs of the *bakirkhani* into the tea.

'The army killed her husband Showkat a year ago…' Abdus Salaam said and paused for a long while. Salaam's daughter reclined her back against the pillar and looked away silently, her face now enveloped in gloom. The baby giggled.

'Showkat didn't even see his son,' Abdus Salaam ruffled the boy's hair. 'Wasim was born three months after.'

The baby prattled.

'It was a fake encounter. They put a Kalashnikov and two hand grenades on him and declared it as a "huge success" on TV.'

Haleema stopped at a sip. The *bakirkhani* had sucked in the whole cup of tea, and had now swollen and risen to the top.

'Showkat was a tailor…he worked in his own shop outside his

home...worked well and earned enough. One evening, he stayed back after his apprentices left; he had to finish a bridal trousseau... late that night some troopers came to his shop and told him they needed to speak to him. He obeyed...he had to – one has to – they bundled him into a Gypsy... Seven days later a navy-blue police truck delivered his body at the bus stop outside the *mohalla*... Showkat had never even uttered the word "gun" ever.'

Haleema let out a long sigh. The day had grown ashen.

'My daughter is a widow now. Her in-laws are from a humble background...' Salaam continued. 'Since Showkat was their sole son among four daughters, he was the only bread earner... His father is old and senile... Looking at their fate I called her home to ease them of some burden.'

The girl was quiet, still looking away and diddling with the tapering end of her plaited hair.

That night she saw Imran in her dream:

He sits on a bench in Valley Hiardressers, waiting his turn for a haircut. His face is hidden behind a film magazine with two dolphins jumping out of an ice-blue sea on its cover. A barber turns around to call Imran. The barber is Abdus Salaam.

Haleema enters the shop and tries to persuade Imran to come home. He refuses with a jostle and frees himself as she grasps his arm. 'You didn't look for me in the places where I was,' he tells her.

'Where didn't I look for you, my son? I looked everywhere, I searched for you like a mad woman. In all the places. Everywhere!' Haleema tells him.

Imran pulls open the shop door and darts away, outside, on the road. Haleema chases after him. He keeps running until he disappears into a shady grove of poplars across the road. She screams out his name but he doesn't reply; she feels her screams are muted. She tries harder, her screams grow louder, but he still cannot hear her.

In an instance, a high, barbwire-topped wall comes up between Haleema and Imran. She tries to climb the wall, but she slips and tumbles down, hitting the ground.

She woke up, bathed in sweat, repeatedly muttering, 'I looked for you! I looked for you everywhere...'

Next morning, Haleema tried her best to enter the Badami Bagh Cantonment, but the troops at the gate did not allow her in. They coldly told her no one was detained at the cantonment. She returned home and packed a basket for Rehbar Khan, Jana's son: some boiled eggs, a fried chicken, a creel blanket, a plastic bag of almonds and a jar of honey. Then she boarded a bus to Lal Chowk; getting off at Exchange Road, she took another bus to Soura where the hospital was, where Rehbar had been admitted.

The army had cordoned off the road to Soura. Just an hour ago a grenade had been lobbed on a patrolling party. It had missed its target and badly injured two pedestrians. Paces away, at Regal crossing, another battalion was already bringing out the men.

The conductor of the bus, which Haleema boarded, overloaded the bus with passengers, whistled and shouted the call to the driver to leave. Standing crammed in the aisle of the bus, people leaned over the seated passengers. There were chit-chats between the passengers. Familiar words were stuck to each lip and tongue: crackdown, fire, grenade, gun, bunker, interrogation, cordon, curfew, I-card, militant, military. At Kralkhud crossing, another posse of army men stopped the bus and yelled at the male passengers, asking them to get down. They queued the men up. Then a trooper stepped into the bus with a black Alsatian on a leash. It sniffed about everything and barked. But as it tried to move near the women and children, who were looking at the trooper and his dog with frightful eyes, the trooper pulled it back with effort, as though it were the dog walking the trooper. The army checked their I-cards, likening the faces with the pictures on the cards.

A man was separated from the line of men and slapped hard on the cheeks. It appeared as if he had forgotten his I-card at home. The other male passengers were ordered to wait half a kilometre ahead to board their bus again. The troops wanted to detain the man but Haleema mobilized other women passengers and intervened. They finally let the boy go.

Beyond the large military outpost beside the dusty compound wall of the hospital at Soura, the road bent and ultimately ended into a crossway at the gate of the hospital. Haleema disembarked under the 'Emergency' porch; attendants of the admitted patients reclined against wilting cedars and rotting thujas in the untrimmed garden. Empty tiffin boxes and large flasks of tea surrounded them. Rice was strewn everywhere.

Limbless, spastic, sick and shaggy beggars sat on the footpath, holding out their laminated prescriptions and pitiable testimonials. A man in a filthy white peasant's cap sold mashed chickpea with *lavaasa* and yogurt chutney with onion, his fingers dirty from the mash. Haleema walked past all of them to where the ambulances were parked. The ambulances looked archaic, the dents on them revealing rusty spots where the white paint had scraped off. They seemed to have been in use forever.

In the emergency ward, an aproned maid was discarding a bin filled with used syringes, broken tinted vials, discarded plastic tubes, bloodied cotton swabs and swathes of pus-smeared bandage.

'Where are the torture victims kept?' Haleema asked her.

'They are everywhere in the hospital. There are two hundred and forty admissions as of now. Who do you want to see?' she said brusquely, as if she had been annoyed with the same question by others before Haleema.

'Rehbar Khan; he is a Gujjar boy from Kupwara. He had been admitted yesterday. His mother is with him,' Haleema said.

'Yesterday's admissions are in the next ward, I mean the emergency ward. You don't have to search the whole hospital. This way, right turn.'

They were running short of beds in the emergency ward. Two patients shared a bed in one corner, and a few just rested against the walls. Haleema found Rehbar and Jana sitting on the floor in a corner. A long transparent plastic tube went into Rehbar's wrist under a crisscross of white adhesive strips. He was lying on a worn-out blanket, resting his nape on Jana's *pheran* that was now roughly folded as a pillow. With his yellow admit card, Jana was fanning off the flies gathering on Rehbar's body. He looked paler than the other day.

'The doctors say his right kidney has nearly failed,' Jana said. 'And his wounds have been severely infected. They say they've cleaned the wounds as much as they can, but there are more serious cases than his, so they've asked me to take him home, put him on a course of medicines and bring him back after twenty days or so for a checkup. But even now he is burning with fever. He is too weak to even hold a glass of water. Just a second…' Jana snapped the conversation on a gesture from her son. With a sudden flick of her body she stood up and lifted Rehbar. He wanted to be helped to the toilet. Haleema assisted Jana. They languidly walked him to the closest washroom. 'They forced him to piss on a red-hot heater. He has been passing blood in his urine since then,' Jana whispered sideways to Haleema.

Back in the ward, Haleema brought out the basket. 'Here. I have got you some things,' Haleema said, bringing out the boiled eggs, chicken, the creel blanket, the plastic bag full of almonds and the jar of honey.

'So nice of you. You are doing much for us,' Jana said. 'I can't return such a gift!'

'It is very little, in fact. I am sorry I couldn't get more,' Haleema said.

'Oh! I am indebted,' Jana felt speechless. 'Come to our place in Kupwara someday,' she invited Haleema, 'give my name to anyone in Dardpora – you will be led to my house. Give me a chance to serve you.'

'Yes, I will, *Insha'Allah*, after your son is healthy again,' Haleema said and left.

That evening at home, Haleema noticed that the garden tap had begun to drip. She cut a strip of rubber from an old bicycle tube and wound it around the tap. Many such puncture-ridden tubes hung by a peg in the backyard shack. Then she realized that the gas had run out. The lighter repeatedly emitted sparks but the burner of the stove just did not react.

At night she went to her bedroom to take her medicine. She stopped in the middle of the corridor only to remember that the particular strip of tablets – the anti-histamine steroids – she took just before going to bed had run out as well. She discovered creases on her face and neck in the fragment of a mirror she kept near her pillow. *I am an old woman now*, she thought, touching her sagging cheeks.

On a drizzly afternoon, Haleema put the chain-hasp on the wooden gate, padlocked it and left for Dardpora.

Dardpora, the abode of pain, was around a hundred kilometres to the west. The village sat along a belt of serene mountains that marked the border with Pakistan. Haleema took a bus that was almost full and ready to leave from the Batamaloo bus stop. She found an unoccupied seat near two other women.

The bus overloaded itself with nearly two hundred passengers – some of whom were sitting on the roof of the vehicle. Baubled *kaangers* hung from the roof rack. The bus conductor pushed himself along the aisle to collect his fair. One of his hands grabbed the bus's support beam and the other held a grooved stack of varied currency notes in ascending order: fivers, tenners, fifties, then a few hundreds.

The highway led through rustic swathes of paddy fields and lush green meadows tracting far and wide, with dense forests in the background. Through the window on her side, Haleema watched men and women working in their fields. They had folded the sleeves of their pyjamas up to their thighs and their hands were soiled and legs sullied by mud. The bus passed by miles of apple orchards, gushing streams and old mud-plastered shops with wooden shutters. The shops were incongruously smothered by chains of potato chips and sachets of cheap shampoo. Communal taps dotted the road on every mile, where women and young girls were washing clothes or filling their pots and dented pitchers.

Passengers were called out and frisked at countless army checkpoints on the way. Except for their bus, the only other vehicles she saw on the road were endless numbers of armoured army vehicles and a few horse-pulled carts.

The bus lurched its way up towards a plateau, the gears hissing and the vehicle straining itself with the load. It pulled up around a blind turn, and a scenic panorama loomed into view. *That's a relief,* Haleema thought, letting the fresh breeze wash past her face. Sprawling houses in the valley of Dardpora huddled together like villages unto themselves. Their tin roofs twinkled brashly in the sun. They looked like soldered electronic circuits from distance. Far away, between the land and the cloud-dashed, pine-furred mountains, a vast lake stretched from the north to the south. Its waters glistened like molten silver in the sunlight. Further away, a man rode a white horse down a mountain towards the lake.

The bus driver played a tape of a classic Kashmiri *shashrang,* a poem in six verses, in the voice of Ghulam Ahmad Sofi:

Yaavan aeses tanna naavan tai, haavas chhuna chhaavaan
Ba wana kaeit gayi ath havaan tai, yi chhu duniya taavan

In my youth I bathed, open secret's charm doesn't last long,
I'll tell how many passed alone, this world doesn't last long.

The bus rolled on through another village. Now Haleema saw long rows of clothes lines heavy with drying clothes inside fenceless compounds. People worked their vegetable farms. The bus stopped to drop a passenger. A woman filling her pitcher at a community tap saw Haleema look at her and passed a courteous smile.

Haleema smiled back.

The tape recorder continued to play:

Ba chhes na vetraavaan tai, taa chhuna kanh ti yivaan
Milvan chha mea te tas kithatravan tai, luukh chhim matczraavaan

No one comes and endure I do not,
Communion knots us, people untie the knot.

The bus entered a secluded, quaint area, and the road seemed to pass through a structure that looked like a wide compound flanked by two strange mud-and-brick houses with numerous windows.

Haleema's fellow passenger was a woman from Dardpora. She wore a choker of red Ladakhi beads that looked like pomegranate seeds, with a dozen matching red bangles on each wrist. Under her floral kameez she wore a men's inner. She had been trying to strike a conversation with Haleema and when she noticed the latter's curious looks at the two houses, she decided now was a good time to do so.

'First time here?' she asked Haleema.

'Yes,' she responded, regarding the woman with interest.

'Then you must know that this is an army camp and not a house. No one lives here. The troops have diverted the road and made it pass through this camp. Gents have to get down, wait and see…' the woman pointed at the men in the bus. As soon as she said the words somebody blew a shrill whistle from outside the bus. All the men inside the bus seemed to be familiar with the whistle, and got down for the parade.

When the men were frisked and paraded, the bus slowly pulled out of the lawn. One of the buildings was strangely constructed; its backside was open, without any doors. It looked as if there was a factory or a mill inside, with giant wheels and belts all over the place.

'You know,' the woman told Haleema, 'they have a bandsaw here, the army.'

'What do they do with a bandsaw?' Haleema asked.

'What does one do with a bandsaw? Don't you see that yellow tarpaulin?' the woman said and cautiously beckoned to a corner. Some large logs of cedar timber peeked out from under the tarpaulin.

'Don't be surprised. They saw everything here, from trees to human beings,' the woman added.

The other side of the camp was fenced in a grid of equidistant barbwire. Empty wine bottles lay suspended from it and tinkled even in the gentlest of breezes. A trooper slid the spiky iron barricade aside and lifted the thick coil of barbwire to let the bus exit.

All of this was a new, shocking revelation for Haleema. *Do they do this in the city camps too? Do they saw the boys? No, no, that can't be.* She tried to dismiss the thought as soon as it clouded her mind.

'Where do you come from, by the way?' the woman asked nobly.

'Natipora, Srinagar,' Haleema said.

'I have never been to Srinagar,' the woman remarked.

'But you boarded the bus from Batamaloo. That is where Srinagar is,' Haleema said, amused.

'I had gone to that place just to get a consignment of *kaangers*. We sell them here. But I never knew it was in Srinagar. What a mystery life is!' the woman said. 'And who are you visiting here?'

'Jana Akhtar. Her son Rehbar Khan has recently been released. Everyone knows her here…'

'*Khudaya*!' The woman exclaimed. 'Sister, you are very late… Rehbar was killed in an encounter just nine days ago.'

'*What*?' Haleema was stunned. She slightly thumped her chest and bit the tip of her tongue. 'But he was released only fifteen days ago. And he had an RO with him – the army had formally let him go.'

'Aah, that is what an encounter is,' said the woman. 'I know he had just been released. But that is no criterion here for not picking a person up again.'

'And the release order? What about that?'

'The army snatched it back a few days before the encounter, so as to give out the impression that he was still active as an insurgent. People met him after he had been released. He was all right and had begun to stroll down the countryside, greeting everyone he met, exchanging pleasantries,' the woman told her.

Haleema sighed.

'After killing him, the savages threw his body in the forest. It was found by a local shepherd... *Khudaaya*! Rehbar's mother put her breast to him to feed him for the last time. The crowd really had to pull her off him. It was like Karbala there. Don't ask me to say anything more...'

A sudden pain began to cramp Haleema's chest and spread to her left arm. She was now scared to face Jana, shuddering at the prospect.

The bus unloaded all its passengers in a small market and drove off.

Haleema stood at the stop for a while, confused, indecisive and worrying about her pain. The sun was right overhead but not as baking as it would have been in Srinagar. Its warmth was pleasant and soothing. One other bus was leaving for Srinagar, with yawning passengers already inside it. Without further contemplation Haleema boarded it.

When Haleema arrived at the house, the muezzins had just announced the call for *magrib*, the evening prayer. She was unsteady on her feet from the long bus journey. Her mind was full of noises and dark thoughts. She sat inside the bathroom on a low wooden stool to perform ablutions for the *magrib*. Some wet patches on the dry cement surface of the bathroom had morphed into ghostly shapes, creating an optical illusion. She studied them with awe. A ghostly figure with a wide-open mouth seemingly shouted back at her. She poured a mug of water and spoiled them all.

She unrolled the prayer rug in her bedroom and tossed her *tasbeeh* in front of it. The prayer rug had the Kaaba stitched in black, flanked by two white minarets. Haleema sobbed in her prostration. Her tears streamed down and fell on the rug. Suddenly, her mind was full of despair and frustration. *This is not going anywhere*, she thought. She had put everything at stake, spent all her time searching for Imran. She had stalled everything. The Joo house had begun to collect dust and cobwebs. She had believed that she would clean it once Imran was home. But everything seemed frozen in time.

11

The fall

With no one left to take care, the house had fallen to shambles.

Haleema resolutely wound her old scarf around her face, wielded a broom, squatted and swept the floors of the house room by room. She stacked the cushions in every room and opened the windows to let out the dust that had gathered in the crevices and chinks. As she demolished the cobwebs under the wooden ceiling, the brooding spiders fled towards the walls. Haleema did not touch them. A robust gale ran through the house and scattered the collected lint from the dustpan here and there. She sat on the bare floor and sighed. Then she did it all over again.

After every minute she would take out the inhaler from her pocket and pump it thrice into her mouth, take a little rest and get going again.

She straddled the heavy, fusty druggets on the compound's wall and beat the dust out of them with a long poplar branch. Then she went inside and picked up the disinfectant from the bathroom, but she couldn't read the instructions on the bottle. Imran alone knew the ratio of the disinfectant to the water. She put the bottle back on the shelf in the bathroom. Then she went mopping, scraping and rubbing stubborn stains vigorously. She scratched the kitchen floor and coated the oven with viscous Multani mud water.

Her back ached now, and she reclined against the kitchen wall, gasping. She didn't touch Ab Jaan's or Imran's rooms. *What if Imran suddenly came from behind and covered my eyes with his hands?* Haleema imagined. One evening, as she laid out the utensils to serve herself dinner, she ladled the rice onto two plates. Then suddenly, while serving the collard, she stopped, and sat down on the wooden stool in the corner of the kitchen. She began to sob, followed by a low wail that reverberated in the empty house.

She only spent nights at the house now. At times, she couldn't even force herself to sleep or wake up from a nightmare. She would then put on her *pheran*, go out into the compound and clear the poplar foliage that had scattered along the walls.

One day, she went to see her cow and its heifer; Shafiqa now took care of them at Haleema's request. The heifer lay snoozing on the ground but the cow recognized her at once and began to moo loudly over and over. She even lashed out at Haleema with her tail. Haleema rubbed between her horns and gently patted on her sides. The animal's eyes filled with tears. Haleema kept wiping hers with the corner of her dupatta, crying silently.

'I am broke. I don't have a penny now,' Haleema told the Imam, sobbing. 'But I have hope. I wish to die but this hope pulls me back. I have spent everything looking for him. I have not let my feet rest anywhere. It seems I have just walked and walked all my life. After Ab Jaan, I have only one reason to live and that is Imran. I don't know what will happen to me. I might faint and fall on a burning stove someday or I might not wake up one morning. But while I exist in this world, I have one reason to live.

'I need your help. I need some money. If you could help me sell my orchard…I don't need that land now. Ab Jaan would take care of it, prune the trees, spray pesticide. After him…any disfigured fruit that grows rots untouched. Even my cattle are gone.

'Animals have breached the fence of the orchard. I have no time and energy left to keep them off. Dogs. Stray cows. I have to clean their droppings every morning. And then there are the trees. The leaves fall in autumn. It breaks my back to sweep them off.

'I want to sell it because I can't take care of it anymore. And I need some money to live on till I find him.'

The Imam gave her an honest listen. 'Go home, I'll do something. You don't have to worry,' he assured her.

After some days he came to the house with three men. One was a prospective buyer and the other two were land revenue officers. One of the revenue officers unrolled a long measuring tape from a black plastic spool and gave the end of the tape to his colleague. He went to the edge of the land, walking and shoving the tall weeds out of his way with a stick. He almost disappeared in the grass where the land began to slope downwards. The Imam called on Haleema and asked her to witness the measurements.

The other revenue officer noted down all the measurements. Then the two officers and the Imam squatted in the middle of the orchard and began discussing the calculations. Haleema watched them intently. The three began to bicker, then a round of bargaining started. The Imam excused himself after a while and came towards Haleema in the verandah.

'They want three and a half lakhs, I am saying five. What do you say?' he asked her.

'As much as you deem is reasonable. I will honour your decision,' Haleema decided.

The Imam sold the land for four lakhs.

Haleema scrawled her signature at the bottom of crisp stamp papers. The very next day, trucks started depositing stones, bricks and sand in the orchard. Then one morning the new owner of the orchard came with a platoon of masons and men and got a plinth built between the house and the orchard.

Haleema watched curiously from behind the kitchen's windows as the men laid brick over brick on the plinth till the orchard disappeared from view. Only the top branches of the plum trees were visible now.

In the waiting hall of a chest specialist's clinic, Haleema was astonished to see a man she hadn't expected to come across. She regarded him in utter disbelief. The man was none other than her husband.

There were other dismayed patients waiting for their turns – all seated on a long wooden bench between Haleema and her husband.

He looked much older than Haleema, much gaunter. Much of his hair had fallen. The remaining few wispy strands had become salt and pepper. All his handsome features had waned.

Haleema's face took an expression full of panic and surprise. She tried to ignore him but the more she did, the more glances she stole at him. He seemed to have already seen her while she had not been aware of his presence. And now that they had seen each other, he put great effort to remain inconspicuous. After so many years, they were together again, separated by an uncomfortable silence and a row of seven impatient patients. Haleema's memory went back to the day when they had posed for the picture. How strange the difference between the two days. Separated by long years of separation, mistrust, catastrophe, misfortune, tribulation and much else.

His long fits of hoarse coughing made him seem more than merely old. Instead, he looked sick and dejected. Haleema observed that he was dressed shabbily, wearing a combination she never expected him to wear – a dirty navy-blue jacket, mint-green pants and unpolished tan leather shoes. She noticed his struggle to disappear at that moment. His turn came and he went straight into the doctor's cabin without looking anywhere else.

When he came out, he nervously fumbled with his shoes, trying to change into them as quickly as possible. His hands were shaking and he was breathless. While walking out, he tripped over a plank of wood fixed on the bottom of the doorframe. Haleema's tongue slipped when everyone said the holy word 'bismillah' when he tripped. She chewed away half the word. Part of her wanted him to trip and fall and the other didn't.

He didn't dare look back and was gone.

Afterwards, Haleema would marvel at the old, cobwebbed memories the encounter brought back, and left her with a new curiosity about his fate. She wondered whether she would see him again at the doctor's clinic or at some market or somewhere else.

12

The jails

There was a slight knock on the door. Haleema was frying potatoes, and the hiss from the pressure cooker drowned out the sound of the knock. After a moment, the knocks grew harder and she strained her ears to ascertain whether someone was at her door – visitors were rare now. And yet, when someone knocked at the door, she would quickly feel her heart sink. Her brain would bellow over and over, *It is him, maybe it is him.* She would get weak in the knees; her hands would tremble – just as they did right now.

What if it is him…

She turned the gas knob with a shivering hand to simmer the flame, leaving the ladle over the frying slices of potatoes, and walked through the small corridor that seemed a thousand miles long. She widened her eyes to look at the person through the netted door. It was Izhar, the BBC journalist.

'What a surprise.' she told him, opening the door. 'After so many days. What a pleasant surprise!' Her bloodshot ears began turning pale again and the thumping inside her chest lowered.

Minutes later Izhar found himself awkwardly sitting under a mink blanket.

'I have an acquaintance in the police. He is posted at the Central Jail. Yesterday, he told me about a young boy he had seen in jail. I didn't pay much attention to what he was saying before he told me his name – Imran,' Izhar told Haleema. She had already begun pouring him tea and stopped midway when he said the name.

'I asked my friend to describe him. When he did, the hair on my neck rose. He then said that the inmate – I mean the boy – might be shifted to some other jail. I thought I must tell you before it's too late. Do go tomorrow and check out. Also, do give me the number of the telephone nearest to you, of any close neighbour, where I can call you, just in case.'

The Central Jail of Srinagar sat in the lap of Mount Hari Parbat. Its premises were surrounded by a twelve-feet-high stone wall, topped off with a six-tier barbwire. Army troops guarded the entry at its high gates, while police personnel, wearing *pherans* and khaki pants, sat splayed on a low wooden bed, basking in the weak spring sunlight in front of the guardhouse near the gate. The gate had a smaller door in it, and one had to watch one's head and clamber over it at the same time while entering.

A *munshi*, a police officer who kept record of the FIRs, sat reclining on a wooden chair inside the jail. The plywood surface of the table he was sitting behind had chipped off along the edges. There was a jagged register on the table, surrounded by rubber stamps and a large stamp-pad. A cheap pen was tethered to a nail on the table's side with a nylon string.

'*Assalaam-u-Alaiqum*, *munshi* sahib,' Haleema greeted him.

The *munshi* opened his right eye first, then the left one and pulled himself upright. He seemed to be irritated at this interruption of his mid-day nap.

'*Bihiv,* sit,' he said.

Haleema sat on one of the two wooden chairs and placed a picture of Imran on the table.

'Has this boy been here?' she eagerly asked him. He took the picture and held it close to his eyes for a while and then put it back on the table.

'Yes. I think once. But what happened?' he asked, narrowing his eyes.

Haleema narrated the full version.

'When did you see him? Do you know anything about him?' Haleema frantically asked him.

'*Humsheera*, I am not sure if the boy I saw in this jail was your son, although he resembles the boy in the photo. I also don't remember when I saw him. But he was definitely here a few days ago. I think he was shifted either to Udhampur jail or sent to Tihar. I shall give you a suggestion: you must look in other jails too. And from each of the jails where you don't find him, you should seek a signed letter confirming his absence. It might help you later. That is all I can tell you now,' the *munshi* advised.

Hundreds of boys were detained by the army every day in the valley, overcrowding the local jails and detention centres. Those who had languished in their dark and rat-infested cells for more than a month were shifted to jails outside the valley to make space for new arrivals. Those shifted out would suddenly discover a new life when they saw daylight once again. As the bright sunlight streamed in through the steel-mesh windows of the army trucks carrying them, the handcuffed boys would let the rays hurt their eyes willingly.

Prisoners were shifted to jails as far as Tihar in Delhi. Their parents followed them with washed and ironed clothes and essential things for daily use, and, above all, to get a glimpse of their sons. Someone or the other would leave for the Indian mainland almost every week to visit their child.

Haleema was looking for one such family who wished to go visit their son, and when Shafiqa and her husband Muhammad Rafiq decided to visit Shaheen in Tihar, she readily agreed to accompany them. She packed a blanket, soap, a pair of nylon slippers, her toothbrush with its worn-down bristles, medicines, a pair of shalwar-kameez and a few kilos of apples.

As Haleema ambled towards the street's end that led towards the Natipora shrine, a figure caught her eye. *Unbelievable*. It was him – her husband. Frail and ill, he was crouching along a wall. His sparse hair was wet and swept backwards. He was wearing an old, oversized tweed coat and navy-blue pants. And unpolished shoes.

When he spotted Haleema, he fumbled to move away. He went as far down the main road as he could to avoid her. She ignored him. She managed a hard look but in her heart she was scared of following him. She was curious about him: whether he simply wanted to talk to her or just wanted to see her or wanted to tell her something she didn't know. She wondered if he knew what had happened.

Muhammad Rafiq and Shafiqa were waiting for Haleema at the shrine. They had hired a white Ambassador car for their journey to Jammu, from where they would take the train to Delhi. The driver of the taxi stacked the luggage on the roof. Shafiqa and Haleema sat in the back seat and Rafiq took the front seat, beside the driver. Haleema sat close to the window, a little away from Shafiqa. She transferred her medicines, money and apples into a small bag that she placed on her lap.

Outside, the morning grew steadily clearer. Haleema noticed the orange orb pitching up from the east, from behind the mountains of Tral, making the dew sparkle on the fields and meadows spanning acres and acres of flat land.

The driver stole quick glances from the highway towards the wheel to sort out an audio cassette from a stack on the dashboard. He finally inserted one; the voice of Fayaz Sheikh boomed from the stereo, backed by the melody from a *tumbaknaer* – an earthen tube closed at one end with sheepskin.

Rafiq immediately scolded the driver for playing music. As the driver reached for the 'Stop' button, Haleema stopped him.

'Let it be.'

Fayaz Sheikh continued to croon.

Past Pampore, the road parted vast saffron fields into two infinite expanses. Women were depositing fresh dung along the mounded rows of saffron beds. The road now seemed like a long, endless sentence, punctuated by bunkers and check posts at bridges, and curves and turns and crossroads. The traffic of words had lost its flow.

The taxi passed by stacks of unfinished cricket bats displayed along the road under shady willow groves at Awantipora. Haleema let the dry and gritty morning air calm her. All the way the thought that her husband had followed her disturbed her. A group of men with prayer caps sat behind a conspicuous green box at a shrine. The car swerved and stopped close to it. Passengers who passed this spot were supposed to pay a *nazrana* for good luck. Haleema held out a rolled fifty-rupee banknote through the window.

These men have collected crores in the name of the shrine for decades, and the shrine looks superb – fine architecture in walnut wood, grand chandeliers, etc. But where does the rest of the money go? Haleema thought. She abruptly said, 'We must help the poor and needy rather than give to these thugs.'

Rafiq turned his head in surprise. For a moment Haleema felt that she would be thrown out of the car and left behind for such a contemptuous comment. Silence followed; a pensive analysis of Haleema's thoughts.

'I think she is right,' Rafiq said firmly. 'Where *has* all the money gone?'

The morning was sunny and radiant now. They stopped for tea at Qazigund, where waiters from roadside restaurants and tea stalls called out non-stop, 'Chai! Chai! Chai!' The three went to a stall where men were drinking their teas with steaming samosas. Haleema washed her hands in a dirty washbasin squeezed into a corner. Mushy blue suds of detergent dotted the sink. The tap's silver gild had half-eroded, revealing spots of bronze. Haleema was subconsciously taking note of all these things for it was the first time she was travelling outside the valley.

It took them five minutes to reach Lower Munda, a check post on the skirting edge of the majestic Pir Panjal range. The driver got off and showed his papers to an officer sitting in a wooden booth beside the road. Then he thumbed a folded note into his palm. The officer tore off a pink receipt and handed it to the driver to let him pass.

The rest of the journey was hilly. As the car pulled up to the Upper Munda summit, Haleema looked out her window over a valley that was now looming into her sight. The check post that had once seemed huge from near now looked like a nippy toy crane. The houses in the valley of Verinaag, the origin of the river Jehlum, grew smaller and smaller as the car climbed higher and higher. The other side of the highway was lined with parked trucks and oil tankers. Helpers washed the windscreens or put stones behind the rear wheels to stop the vehicle from moving, while the drivers slept inside.

Troops stopped the taxi at the mouth of the Banihal tunnel and got them to line up in a long queue of vehicles. They called out the passengers and frisked them thoroughly. While the troops fished Rafiq's pockets, Haleema saw that his conical pockets, turned inside out, looked like a street bitch's nipples: fluff, dust, paper crumbs and powdered remains clung to them. The troops unlocked the boot and reined in a salivating dog to sniff the baggage.

Haleema thought of Ab Jaan – she was surprised, for she'd thought of him after a long time. *How would he have felt had it been him accompanying me to find Imran? What would he say to the humiliation he would have faced to pass a tunnel he had once worked to build? Would the troops have trusted him and honoured him for his work and let him go?*

After a thorough search, the troops allowed them to sit in the taxi. It took two more hours before the taxi could enter the tunnel, the long unending jam marked by honks and exhaust smoke. Netted bulbs glowed from the walls of the tunnel. At some point water dripped from the ceiling. A blinding speck of light from the other end swelled and swelled as the car approached it until they finally got out of the tunnel and the valley.

The car danced over a bad patch of the highway below Patnitop where a landslide had eaten away the road, which now went through serpentine curves and above a valley floor that was thousands of metres below them. Haleema looked down at the deep ravines they had to pass.

A roofless truck filled with cowering, turbaned labourers lumbered up the road just ahead of their taxi. It threw up clouds of sandy dust and noxious smoke behind it. Haleema rolled up her window and asked the others to do the same.

While Shafiqa droned on and on, with no one particularly, Haleema became disinterested. She had quietly excused herself from Shafiqa's monologue and devoted her attention to the surroundings. *I can never forget this journey*, she thought. *I can never forget its purpose*.

At Kud, the traffic slowed down to a snail's pace. A crowd had gathered around a bend on the road, and passengers had got off their vehicles to look down the deep gulch. Haleema caught a glimpse of an overturned oil tanker. They overheard a few people discuss that an army truck had rammed into it head-on. The wreckage of the tanker lay several metres away from the spot of the accident.

The tanker had left behind a bruised trail of rocky scree on the ridge. At the site of the accident, broken glass lay scattered on the road like table sugar, while tyre marks now smelt of burnt rubber. Their taxi almost hurtled out of the messy spot.

More roadside junkyards full of discarded giant, rusty machines and bent metal now dotted the highway.

Travel-beaten, they reached Udhampur just when the sun had begun to rise on the other side of the world. They turned right at a crossroad and geared up to climb a hillock, on top of which was the jail. It was the first jail on their way to Tihar, and they had decided to check whether Imran was here or not.

The road to the jail took them through dense overgrown thickets and bushes. The hard thorny branches scratched the hull of the car as it crossed through. They were still metres away from the giant gate when an invisible guard blew his whistle. '*Gaadi wahin pe roko*! Stop the car,' he hollered.

They stopped. Haleema saw that there was another gate more massive than the first inside the premises of the jail, half-a-kilometre away from where they had halted.

She asked the guard, who came out of his invisible post, if they could go inside.

'It is too late. Visits close at three in the afternoon. Come tomorrow,' he said calmly, hanging onto the driver's window, his hand tenderly tapping the roof of the car. His eyes made a detailed survey of the car and of the people inside it. When the driver started the car again, the guard reluctantly pulled himself off as though he wanted to remain there, motionless, bending over the window for the whole night.

They drove back to town, deciding to spend the night in Udhampur and visit the jail next morning. They checked into a mediocre hotel called Hill View. It was next to a motorcycle showroom and the Police Training Academy. The driver and Rafiq slept in one room and the women in the other. It seemed as if they were the only guests the hotel had in a long time; the hotel seemed empty apart from them. Mice had eaten into their quilts, and the cotton stuffing had begun to bleed from the holes. Haleema said it was futile to complain at that late hour; wisdom lay in passing the night and not spending it awake. 'Since Kashmiris are unwelcome everywhere outside of our lands, a complaint might harm us more.'

Yet, Haleema rolled about in bed the whole night. The pillow smelt of stale alcohol; the stench didn't let her sleep.

They quickly checked out in the morning and left to visit the jail. The same guard greeted them. He descended down an oblique path towards the car. 'I hate the way he stared at us yesterday,' said Shafiqa.

'Ogled at us instead,' Haleema quickly corrected her.

'Yes. Exactly,' said Rafiq.

But this time, the guard did not hang on to the window. He called the driver outside, put his arm around his neck and then took him aside. He gesticulated and smiled, and gesticulated and smiled again. The driver responded with a quizzical regard and a reluctant smile.

The trooper left the driver behind and walked back towards the jail.

'What?' everyone asked the driver after he joined his passengers.

'He says that since we are Kashmiri, he cannot allow us to visit the jail. He says he has strict orders not to allow any Kashmiris. But he can allow us to meet the chief warden…but we would have to go on foot…inside…provided…'

'Provided what?' Haleema asked impatiently.

'Provided we provide him with a crate of apples and a kilo of almonds or walnuts.'

The packet of Burzali almonds that Shafiqa had carried for Shaheen in Tihar was given to the guard. 'We don't have apples. Kindly allow us in now,' begged Haleema.

The guard considered Haleema's request for a while, diddling with the rustling transparent cellophane the almonds were packed in.

'*Theek hai, jao.* You can go,' the guard said quietly a minute later.

They were asked to leave their *pherans* at the gate and were not permitted to carry anything inside. They were given a pass to meet the warden. The driver was not allowed to accompany them.

The three of them sauntered and huffed up the grassy zigzag path. The terraced white barracks of the jail were within sight now. There was no chance any prisoner could run away from a place like this. There were either thick forests or steep ridges on all sides. It was a perfect jail.

The warden was a fat man with a rotund head too big for his body. He was halfway through his huge glass of fresh buffalo milk when Haleema disturbed him. He made gulping sounds as he guzzled it down quickly, surprised at seeing three visitors enter his office.

'We are looking for my son…' Haleema said, placing Imran's picture before him on the table.

'And how do you know he is here?' he asked, letting the last drops of the milk slither down the tumbler onto the flicking tip of his tongue.

'We are not sure but we want to look. Actually…'

He interrupted her.

'Look, let me tell you in plain words… The boy in this picture is not here. He has never been here… We have prisoners of KLF and others who have been here for a long time. That is it.'

'Can we meet one of them?' asked Rafiq.

'No, no. Not permitted. Why? Is this a shop where you ask a shopkeeper to show some other cigarette when the one you want is not available? What the hell! Get out!'

They returned to the hotel, dismayed.

Just before noon, they left for Jammu, where they checked into an ordinary hotel whose name they didn't bother to note. They visited the Central Jail at Heera Nagar after lunch, where again there was no trace of Imran.

They next went to Kuthua Jail, and once again, Haleema returned defeated.

The final destination on this tour of jails was Tihar. Rafiq bought tickets for the three of them in black – second-class sleeper – as all seats to Delhi had been sold out. At Jammu railway station, they searched for their names on a glue-sodden typewritten list pasted on the wall of a blue bogey. The words in the list had swelled and been smudged out, but at least their tickets were confirmed. They tucked their belongings under their seats and sat waiting for the train to honk, squeal and begin the journey to Delhi.

Haleema could see the sparkling bulbs from shops that sold spurious-looking travel bags on the platform. In the coal-black darkness outside, the bulbs were the only needles of light. A few malnutritioned dogs were raking up the garbage from a municipal waste bin, scrounging for whatever they could get. Many passengers were sleeping on the platform against their luggage.

The grandly named Shalimar Express began to chug at nine. It passed through dark villages and open fields, whistling periodically. At midnight, it stopped at an unknown station. Tea vendors hopped in and moved from bogey to bogey with a stack of Styrofoam cups and long flasks of cheap tea. They were followed by peddlers selling spiced peanuts and snacks; then by foggy-eyed beggars, singing songs from old Bollywood films in sweet voices and collecting alms in rotten tin boxes and dented aluminium bowls.

Delhi was radiating with heat. *How hot would it be in prisons here?* Haleema thought. *If he is somewhere here, how can he tolerate it?*

When they introduced themselves as Kashmiris at an ordinary hotel in Paharganj, the receptionist looked up, paused and dropped his pen. 'Sorry, no room is available. Please look in some other hotel,' he said curtly.

Dejected and scared, they had no choice but to travel far to the extremes of north Delhi and look for a vacant, untenanted flat in Azadpur that belonged to Rafiq's friend's friend. But Rafiq didn't know the proper address of the flat. He went to a public telephone booth to call his friend to trace the exact landmark.

The owner of the phone booth sat cross-legged in a chair. He was loading a roll of paper into the billing machine. The goddess Kali sat smugly on a small wooden sanctum, flanked by two lit incense sticks, on the wall behind him. Rafiq entered a narrow kiosk inside the booth and dialled a number. The owner noticed Kashmir's code on the billing machine and cut the call. He hastily put on his slippers and knocked on the glass door of the kiosk.

'Please don't make any calls from here.'

'But why?' Rafiq asked, puzzled.

'I don't want any trouble from the police.'

'But I need to make an urgent call,' Rafiq insisted.

'Okay. But please make sure you leave a copy of your identity card and full details of your residence in Delhi and Kashmir,' he demanded.

Rafiq re-dialled the number several times, but the line was busy. He decided to give up and leave the booth after one last try. As soon as he had prepared to drop the receiver into the cradle, the busy tone gave way to a ring.

The empty flat was on the ground floor of a rundown building in Azadpur: locked, dark and windowless. The keys to the flat were with the neighbours upstairs. Rafiq went to get them while Haleema and Shafiqa waited outside in the narrow lane. He tapped on the first door upstairs and then pressed a small bell, marked 'Bellpush'. A dot of light emerged from the peephole of the door. Then someone peeked outside from the hole. Rafiq heard a quick hush-hush, before a weary old lady in a pinstriped nightie opened the door. She observed him for a considerable while and then went in without speaking to him. Rafiq stood there, motionless. A little while later, a child, dressed in a red vest and white capris, came out with the keys.

The vacant flat was a house without corridors, where the only way to get to one's room was through another's. They spent the whole night lying awake, slapping stubborn mosquitoes against the walls.

They rented a taxi in the morning for Tihar. Midway, at a slum encampment, they halted at a tea stall for breakfast. Repairs were being carried out on the drain along the main road. Worn-down shreds of polythene stuck out from the earthy walls of the drain. Water leaked from a pipeline, and a slum boy was enjoying his morning shower under a parabolic jet from the leakage. A pool of soapy muddy water had gathered around him. His shabby-looking mother squatted atop a wide cement pipe, wherein the two of them lived, and looked on keenly at her son, cupping her cheek in her palm, her elbow resting on her knee, as if in a trance. As if a roadside shower was something precious. Strangely, Haleema envied the woman, despite her evident poverty – she was just an ordinary mother, observing her ordinary son. *It is better to live in a sewage pipe with your son than to live alone in this world!*

The taxi sashayed its way into the rural interiors of the capital city. Here, the houses clung to each other, mimicking coloured cardboard boxes stacked side by side. The taxi continued to go deeper, until it finally reached the village after which the jail was named. A narrow straight track lined with tamarind trees and a grassy side-path led to a monstrously tall and fortified red gate, on top of which the words 'Central Jail No. 1 Tihar' were painted.

Three guards were sitting inside a corrugated tin cabin beside the gate. One of them held his rifle by its barrel between his legs. Another was dozing on a row of assembled stools. The third squashed tobacco in his left palm assiduously. They immediately came to attention when they saw the three of them approaching the cabin.

After thorough questioning, the guards allowed Rafiq to go inside and collect visitors' passes. While he went in, Haleema overheard snippets from the guards' conversation in their accented Haryanvi – 'Kashmiri…terrorist…boy' – while they stole glances at them.

With each passing minute the morning was becoming more and more scalding and hot. Finally, Rafiq walked out with some chits rolled up in his fist. 'Let's go,' he told them.

The gateway that led to the premises of the jail was a dingy and damp squarish tunnel under a building that stank of urine. The path led to the chief warden's office, a man with a handlebar moustache and a gravelly voice. The moustache was the only conspicuous feature on his face. He sat reading a Hindi newspaper whose margins were already dirty with meaningless shapes: rectangular boxes in roughly drawn circles, some crossed-over names in Hindi, and some figures that looked like enlarged asterisks. He had drawn a blue moustache and a beard on a man in a photograph accompanying a news item. On the wall behind him hung a framed photograph of Mahatma Gandhi gazing into eternity from a sky-blue background.

'Sir,' Rafiq asked the warden. 'May we come in?'

The warden folded the newspaper gingerly and put a radio over it.

'Yes,' the warden said in a heavy voice.

Rafiq presented the passes to him.

'Dilip?' he called the guard sitting outside his office. The guard tapped in and corrected his beret.

'Sir?' he asked.

'Take them inside the meeting room and tell Pramod to bring their boy,' he ordered.

They were taken to a room made of two equal chambers. Both chambers were separated by a thick glass wall. On both sides of the glass wall there were microphones connected to a voice recorder. Each side had a separate entry. The chamber they were waiting in had a long bench, and on the other side of the glass wall was a single chair.

After a few minutes, a boy with a wiry body frame and long beard appeared across them. It was Shaheen. He sat on the chair and smiled with difficulty. Rafiq and Shafiqa began to weep quietly. They kissed the glass where Shaheen put his hand. Shafiqa pressed her hand on the glass and wiped it. Haleema smiled and gesticulated at Shaheen. He responded to her and looked puzzled, wondering what Haleema was doing with his parents in that ugly place.

When Shafiqa asked him whether he was well, he smiled wryly and nodded.

'How are you?' Haleema asked him simply.

'Not bad,' he replied quietly and smiled lightly. 'Is everything all right?'

'Yes,' Haleema said.

Rafiq interrupted and narrated the briefest version to Shaheen. He listened with furrowed brows.

'Do you know anything about him?' Haleema asked Shaheen.

'I have not come across Imran. I can never imagine him to be my inmate here. No, not possible at all,' he said.

The siren beeped and a guard walked in. 'Time up,' he announced loudly.

They took an auto-rickshaw back to the flat. The midday sun was beating down on them now, and when the auto stopped at a traffic light, the heat felt even more sapping. They were wet to the bone with sweat. Even the dogs of Delhi had taken refuge in the shade, under parked trucks, buses and carts. Despite the heat, shaggy-haired, lice-ridden beggars and disabled children selling tabloids and small plastic Indian flags came out of nowhere and appeared at the windows of cars. They touched the drivers' elbows resting on the car's window, or voluntarily started dusting bumpers, and then asked for money when the yellow traffic light began to glow.

The heat slapped against Haleema's cheeks. She craned her neck out and looked up at the sky.

13

Khizir Post-mortem

Seasons – winter, spring, summer and autumn – came and went. People kept dying, houses and schools kept crumbling. Bunkers and army camps mushroomed. The valley dwindled. Haleema was oblivious to all. Her search for Imran had become her habit, a habit she couldn't do without. Jails and courts became routine affairs, like going to school. Six days a week she locked the wooden gate at dawn and went to the court. Sundays were official government holidays.

She now knew almost every lawyer, judge, judicial clerk, police officer and journalist in Kashmir. She had knocked on almost all the doors of concerned departments. They all recognized her in turn as well. She now knew relatives of other victims of custodial disappearances too, and could identify terms and jargons of law, journalism, politics and war that she had heard over and over again hundreds of times. She had learnt to use them accurately, even if she mispronounced them: victim as 'vic-tum'; enquiry as 'en-cave-ri'; pamphlet as 'pump-let'; identity became 'aten-ti-ty'; chief minister 'cheap-manish-ter' and government 'goher-mi-nat'.

In a way, this longing, this pain of waiting, was like preparing for hope. This pain of expecting was an education too, an exposure to what life held and meant.

Plop plop plop. It had rained slowly the whole night before. The next day was a windy March Sunday, with perfect spring weather.

The pathway was littered with willow catkins and sticky poplar buds, but Haleema thought she would cook something before clearing the path, something that suited Kashmiri spring.

When she walked down the rain-saddened neighbourhood to the Natipora market for vegetables, the shops were either closed or had half their shutters drawn. Separatists had called for a shutdown of the valley. Some of the shops operated from the back, as Ab Jaan had done. Boys were playing cricket with a banded plastic ball on the road, a wooden stool for stumps and the bowler's end marked by a *kaanger*; lines were drawn with bricks to mark the creases. Haleema walked across their 'pitch' to cross the road. The sun had begun to peep through a gap in the clouds and smile at Natipora. She took a shortcut through an abandoned apple orchard, crossed a pontoon over a small parching stream and arrived at a grocer's. The shop was shut from the front, but the grocer sat in the back with weighing-scales on a flattened burlap sack amid mounds of vegetables and fruits. He was haggling with his customers, mostly women who spent hours bargaining for a discount.

The customers greeted Haleema when they saw her. 'Any news?' a woman asked her.

Haleema calmly shook her head to say no.

'May God bring him back to you very soon! And give you patience,' the woman prayed, consoling Haleema – something she hated. These expressions of consolation and empty sympathy felt like alms given in charity, which she despised.

The grocer quickly attended to Haleema out of turn. Other customers who were waiting acquiesced. But Haleema refused. 'I will wait for my turn,' she said stiffly, despite a storm of insistence.

When her turn came, she picked up a dozen oranges and chose a bunch of soiled *knol khol* and gleaned out a sheaf of mint for her chutney. She gently beat the roots of the *knol khol* against the ground to shake off the traces of earth clinging to them. The grocer didn't charge her for the mint.

A girl from the neighbourhood waited for her outside her house.

She lived a dozen houses away from her. 'What is the matter, dear?' Haleema asked her, smiling, touching the girl's cheek. 'Is everyone at home all right?'

'Yes, everyone is all right… I came twice earlier to call you and found the gate locked. Anyway, you have a call on our phone. It is on hold for the third time now,' the girl informed in a sing-song voice.

Haleema went with the girl, holding her hand in hers while swinging the bag of vegetables from the other hand.

'Who had called?' Haleema asked her.

'He said he was from BBC,' the girl said.

'Oh! It must be Izhar sahib.'

'*Haan*, he said something like that. Papa exchanged wishes with him.'

'Hmm.'

At the girl's house, she led Haleema through a vestibular room into the kitchen. The girl's father welcomed her. Her mother was stoking something in a hissy pan on the stove. She simmered down the flame, left the ladle in the pan and came up to hug Haleema. The air smelt of fried food. Haleema sat near the door, wincing sorely.

'Please come here. You are not supposed to sit at the door,' the father hospitably requested Haleema, gesturing her to sit where he had been sitting, against a sagging cushion.

The telephone receiver was on a low stool near the door of the kitchen. The father picked it up from the tablecloth-covered stool and brought it near her. 'He has been waiting for a long time. He called twice before. Here,' he said, handing the receiver to Haleema.

'Hello!' Haleema said, leaning back against the cushion.

'*Assalaam-u-Alaiqum*. Are you fine?' Izhar greeted.

'*Wa'alayqum ussalaam*! Long life and health to you. Yes, I am fine,' said Haleema.

'I called before as well.'

'Yes, I heard. I was not home.'

'I wanted to tell you that there is an organization called SHRC, the State Human Rights Commission. It is on Boulevard Road.

You must go and register there. It will help make our case stronger,' insisted Izhar.

'Yes, I will. For sure I will, as you say,' replied Haleema.

'Yes. The organization is governmental. But it is important to register there for your case. It will help you.'

The girl's mother was stoking the pan again, while observing Haleema sympathetically.

'Yes, I will. Okay,' Haleema said, ending the call. 'May God give you a long life,' she said in a low voice, but Izhar had already put down the phone.

'He has helped me since the beginning. May God keep him,' she told the parents of the girl, referring to Izhar. The girl watched her quietly.

'May God keep you in good health!' Haleema thanked the family and left, struggling to turn down their insistence on a cup of tea.

The sun dazzled over the untamed horizons of Srinagar's skies the next morning. Haleema went to look for the SHRC on the same road she had once taken to Papa 2. She asked a salesman at the Kashmir Shawl and Carpet Emporium for exact directions. He paused amid praising a pashmina shawl to a few tourists and pointed towards a lane.

She found a bunker at the entrance of the lane and then another at the gate of SHRC. The building was covered in pink stucco. As she climbed the stairs, her back began to hurt. Supporting it with one hand, it took Haleema several more minutes to climb them. Posters were pasted on the walls in a pattern of ascension. A sketch of a hand on one said, 'Stop Human Rights Violations'. Another had a black gun crossed over in red and read, 'Stop the gun'. Finally, at the top of the stairs, one screamed, 'Safeguarding Human Rights Our Duty'.

Haleema was out of breath. She sat on the stairs, clutched the banister in one hand and tried to breathe in as deeply as possible. She took out her inhaler, shook it once and pumped it twice into her mouth.

It seemed to her that the building was empty. No one had come up to look at the visitor. She stood in the gallery once she caught her breath and wondered which door she should knock on. She finally decided and knocked lightly on a door to her right. There was no response. She knocked again, a little harder this time, and the door slowly creaked open on its own, the hinges piping a strange musical note. There was nobody inside; bundles of papers, tightly tied up with jute strings cutting into their worn edges, were stacked everywhere.

She pushed open another door to find a man snoring in a wooden chair that was fixed to the ground, its back draped in a pink towel. The man had his brogued feet thrown over the seat of another chair across him. A dull reflection of the window shone from the shoes, while the man's face was half-covered by his bobbled cap. His arm slipped off the armrest and hung loose in the air until he pulled it up. And then it slipped again.

Haleema didn't disturb him and gingerly walked out, closing the door after her. She finally knocked on the last door in the dark corridor. A steel nameplate proudly announced, 'Chairman'. 'Come in. Come in,' a voice said from the inside. She opened the door and found a child-faced man sitting behind a large table covered with a thick floral spread; the cloth would have made a better curtain. The table was bare, except for an old-fashioned black telephone and an oddly folded newspaper. The man was warming his hands on a coal brazier whose chimney went out a hole punched through a cardboard that substituted as a windowpane. With his tilted astrakhan *karakuli* and an oversized, grey tweed-coat, his perfectly trimmed salt-and-pepper beard and a pencil moustache suited him clearly.

'Please sit down,' he offered Haleema, pointing at a chair in front of him.

She narrated the full version to him. He listened keenly, not interrupting her at all. Then, once she had finished her story, he began.

'Look, I shall tell you something very candidly. Please do not share it with anyone else. This is strictly off the record... We are a state government organization. Our commission is a toothless tiger. At the end of the day we will only be able to register your case and claim for compensation. Not more. Nothing more than that. Don't expect justice from us,' he said honestly.

Haleema smiled.

'Even if you don't claim compensation, you still need a clearance from the mortuary of the police control room to register your case. You will be required to furnish a certificate from the PCR, certifying that they have not received any such body, whose face resembles the picture you show, so far, as proof that your son has not been seen dead and hence could officially, to an extent, be declared missing. You will not go for compensation; I know that from the look on your face. But as an elder brother or father – you choose whatever relation you deem is suitable to you – I will advise you to register here. It will make your case stronger. If not today, maybe someday.'

'Right,' Haleema said.

At the PCR mortuary that evening, Haleema met an inconspicuous, middle-aged coroner called Khizir. Though his full name was Khizir Muhammad, everyone referred to him as Khizir Post-mortem – he had performed over ten thousand post-mortems throughout his service.

The skies had already turned indigo several minutes before sunset. And even when the day transformed to night, Haleema did not worry about being late to reach home. She was answerable to nobody, and nobody worried for her.

Khizir sat in a steel chair, resting his arm on a grubby pad of the wooden armrest, in a shadowy room outside the morgue. He was writing undecipherable words on unevenly torn pieces of paper and sheaving them neatly in the other hand. He was a short man, with a large sallow face full of creases. His cheeks had become pitted, and against those large eyes, the thick nose and the wide mouth, he looked quite comical. His hairline had receded but whatever remained was thick and matty. He wore a long ink-stained white coat over a thick home-knitted woollen pullover, unironed khaki pants and brown unpolished shoes. He carried a mysterious depth in his small eyes.

'I want to talk to you for a moment,' Haleema asked him.

He looked up from his writing and regarded her with a stare for a moment. Then he gestured at her to sit down in another chair. There was a sharp stench of phenyl, which, Haleema thought, hid the smell of the dead.

After some time Khizir stood up and, with a humped back, strutted towards a cupboard, taking one step shorter than the other. He pulled open a drawer and carefully stashed the paper scraps inside it. He pushed the drawer in, locked it and put the bunch of over-used keys – whose notches had almost melted away – into his coat's right pocket, dragging his chair close to Haleema's.

'Yes, what is it?' he asked laconically, his words measured. His voice was as thick and heavy as his limbs.

She took out Imran's picture from a plastic bag and placed it on the pad of his chair's armrest. 'Have you ever seen my son?' she asked. Her heart began to pound.

He studied the picture for a long while, pinched out a filterless cigarette from a green packet and gently stuck it to his pursed old lips. He struck a match, and shielding the stick with his cupped hands, artfully lit the cigarette; his mouth went orange for a moment under the flame. He took a long drag and blew two columns of smoke out of his nostrils.

'No, I don't think so,' he said bluntly. 'But whose picture is this?'

Haleema narrated the full version.

He listened to her story inscrutably, and took a long pause before responding.

'I shall tell you something very important... In this ugly business of the dead, which I have been engaged in for what feels like ages, if you were me, you wouldn't be able to tell whether you have opened and sewn a person or not from a picture. How will you say, "Yes, I have sewed up a particular person who resembles this picture", when the person didn't have a face. I have stitched heads on bodies; heads, which anyway failed to form a face – so defiled, so disfigured. You must bear me out, sister. But I have to tell you that I hardly falter.'

'How can you tell for sure?' Haleema interrupted, needing Khizir to substantiate his explanation for her own satisfaction.

'I have spent years with the dead. Thirty bloody years. I have been so accustomed to them that sometimes I imagine myself lying there, on the cold slab, and conducting my own post-mortem. Frisking my own gut. It is all mechanical to me now, like checking for a leak on a pipe. Or like tailoring – cutting and sewing.'

'I have come to you with hope. I want to believe everything you say, that you have not seen him. Tell me more about yourself, about your work. Not for the certificate but to convince me otherwise,' Haleema said.

'When I got this job thirty years ago, people rushed to greet me. Guests flooded our old drawing room at Safa Kadal. "*Mubarak*! *Mubarak*!" they said. In those days, getting a government job after a paramedical training, and that too in the police, was like going to the moon.

'In the beginning, my hands would tremble and the scalpel would go off the mark. Just touching the skin of the dead would give me jitters. Now, it feels like leather. When I would take home fruits from Jahangir Chowk, my youngest daughter would say that they smelt of the dead, along with my hands.

'All of this didn't bother me till 1989. That year, I lost my sleep. Whatever sleep I got was riddled with nightmares. The bodies at the morgue were everywhere. They invaded my dreams, walking into them unwarranted. A man thanked me once for sewing his bullet-torn face back on his head.

'Then there was a young boy – in whose stomach I found coals and strips of cloth. His gut smelt of kerosene. When I probed his nails I found something sticking to them. The forensic report later said they were traces of his own skin.'

Khizir became garrulous now. 'I have seen worse, much worse. But I don't want to trouble your thoughts. Doctors just come, poke around and then prepare a report. But it is us, post-mortem assistants, who have to be with the dead at all times. I am retiring next year, and I have begun doing something that you might think most absurd: I write a prayer for the dead on these scraps of paper and sign my name beneath their names. It gives me a strange pleasure. I believe the dead will favour me on the Day of Judgment.'

He smiled and took a long pause. 'Anyway, give me the full name of your son and a copy of his photo. I will get the certificate for you tomorrow. Everyone has already left. See, it is getting dark outside,' he said with an apologetic face. His tone changed from blunt to soft. He stamped the cigarette butt on the floor and catapulted the stub outside the window with his forefinger.

'Imran,' said Haleema. 'His name is Imran Joo.'

'Imran. Imran?' asked Khizir, with a little twitch on his face. 'I have recently heard this name… Yes, now I remember! Someone told me yesterday that a Gujjar boy found – please forgive me for saying this – the body of a young boy, believed to have been tortured to death, in the Wular. The body is with the police there and will reach us soon for autopsy. According to the investigation report, something on the body says – I am sorry to say – the boy's name was Imran. God knows.'

Khizir immediately lit another cigarette after this.

Haleema shrivelled with fear and premonition at this news or rumour or whatever it was. She turned pale at once. Her mouth went absolutely dry, her lips almost chapped. She thought that she could not make it back home, let alone walk outside the mortuary to find an auto-rickshaw. She felt uncertain and weaker. As she walked out of that cold room that smelt of death and disinfectant, she began to shake all over. Suddenly the air she was breathing began to feel like cotton, choking her throat. Her mouth was agape and the silence around her turned into a loud whistle in her ears.

The station house officer at the Bandipora Police Station informed Haleema and Shafiqa that the body they wanted to see had been sent to the mortuary in Srinagar. They left the police station and went straight to find the Gujjar boy who had found the body. The two began walking towards Wular lake; it was one of the places where dead bodies who died in custody were said to be jettisoned.

The shepherd Gujjar boy unconditionally agreed to guide them to the foothill where he had come across the body.

'Stay here and take care of the rest,' the boy whispered into the ear of the oldest ram in his drove in Gojri, believing the animal would obey his command. 'I know the place. Come,' he said to Haleema. He took with him an unsteady lamb, holding it against his chest. 'He can't stay without me. I am like his father. His mother died a few days ago,' the boy explained to Haleema in his Gojri-accented Kashmiri. 'Don't step anywhere else except where I walk; it is all marsh and swamp out here, and can easily suck in a person,' he instructed. 'I have seen countless corpses rotting here. I have not spoken about it to anyone.'

'What did the boy look like? His clothes?' Haleema asked the boy.

'His face was a little out of place. Can't say exactly. But, yes, he wore pants and a shirt. I can't tell you the exact colours because his clothes were coated all over with mud. Follow me. I will show you where. Follow me.'

It was an unusually marshy land, without any soul in sight except for the three of them as far as the mist-robed mountains in the north.

They stopped at a gorge, panning their heads left to right and right to left.

'Imran!' Haleema squealed loudly in frustration. The boy looked at her in shock but soon his look became merciful and resolute.

The name bounced back in a lasting echo.

'Imran saeba!' Haleema wailed again.

'Imran saeba...aa...a...' The echo came back.

'Imran!' she howled, this time with a hint of sobbing in her voice.

The hills responded once more.

Birds that had nestled in the tall reeds flew away in V-shaped flocks as they walked past them; a herd of wild horses stopped to drink where the waterline kissed the hills, scraping each other with their muzzles. A filly suckled at a mare's udders.

The boy pressed Haleema's shoulder from behind. 'Be steadfast,' he consoled her. He pointed to a spot where the reeds grew in dense clumps.

She returned home in a dismal state, Shafiqa comforting her all the way.

The next morning, Haleema waited with Khizir outside the morgue to identify the body, shivering, trembling. After sometime, Khizir took her inside. Her heart began to sink further and further, like an anchor that dragged her to the depths of torment.

As Khizir pulled out a drawer, the tremors intensified. He lifted the shroud off the dead boy's face, and she almost began to faint.

But it was not Imran.

14

The Half Mother

A man called Shakeel stood in the wooden witness box of the courtroom in his bathroom slippers. He wore a grey Khan dress, with his nine-inch long jail-grown beard flowing down to his chest. One of his wrists was shackled to a long chain, the other end held by a constable. His free hand rested on the rounded top of the witness box's corner post.

'*Janaab*, soon after our folks were caught in a raid on our hideout, in which his brother Shaheen was caught, Imran Bhat and I began to look for other shelters. We wanted to mislead Major Kushwaha.

'*Janaab*, we knew he was not going to spare us after we had attacked the party that escorted a Pandit who had come to his abandoned home in Natipora. I was caught when we were on the run, but Imran Bhat escaped. I was jumping off the wall of the house we were hiding in, but I fell backwards. I was caught alive and straight away taken to Natipora army camp. Before Major Kushwaha started twisting me, he guffawed and said, "A man means a medal." He tortured me day and night. I asked God for death or freedom from him. When the torture didn't abate, I became an atheist for some days. I decided to distract Major Kushwaha. I told him I knew a boy who was a namesake of Imran Bhat: Imran Joo was on my mind. Major thought about it for a long time. Then one night he suddenly barged into my cell and got me dressed in a long trench coat and wrapped a scarf around my face. We raided Imran Joo's house and caught him. After that raid I was handed over to Papa 2. The last time I saw Imran Joo was in a cell at Badami Bagh. He was scared, but he was fine.'

The court also summoned Abdus Salaam the barber for his version.

Haleema finally decided to file a case against the army. Izhar accompanied her to Advocate Farooq Ahmad. It took Imran's file a month to reach its first hearing. In the following days, on her frequent visits to the court, Haleema would see uncertain and wary-looking men and women – relatives of those who, like Imran, had disappeared – sitting in the back of the courtrooms and patiently waiting for hours together for their respective hearings; while waiting, each watched the other's proceedings: someone's husband, brother, father or son would be missing. Haleema learned that they were going through the same ordeal as she was.

There would be children too, in the courtrooms, with pacifying toys or lollipops in their hands. They were bored by the long discussions, and when they grew restless, they would begin to wail, throw the toys away and wanted to be taken outside. Then there were those children whose fathers had disappeared even before they were born. They recognized their fathers only from the photos their mothers carried. Some children would fall asleep in the middle of proceedings.

As time passed, Haleema jelled with this little society of relatives of disappeared persons. They would all sit together, eat or stroll in the park outside the courtroom and discuss their future actions. Haleema heard all their stories and she told them her own.

As enforced disappearances became routine in Kashmir, the number of relatives swarming the courts for justice increased by the day. The protracted listlessness from the courts forced the relatives to unite.

One day, Haleema voluntarily gathered all the relatives in the park outside the court. Facing the gathering, she reclined against a cement post that held a tubular fencing of steel pipes. A young woman stood next to her with a little son who clasped her burqa with one hand while the other hand was engaged in lifting a half-eaten slab of chocolate wafer up to his lips that were already moustached with chocolate stains. Another old man rested his crossed arms over his knees under his *pheran* and strained himself to listen to Haleema, who loosened the stiff lumbar belt from under her *pheran* – those sitting close to her turned their heads immediately at the muffled crackle of the velcro. 'My belt,' she said, smiling lightly.

The cold of the cement gradually numbed her back, causing her to shift and stand against a lofty larch. Her back had begun to give her real trouble in recent days.

A cold sky hung above them.

'…see, it is getting murkier every day. It is getting difficult to fight individually like this…' she told them. Her hands were joined in her lap. 'But it is also difficult to fight collectively without being formally together. You know what I mean?'

Some heads nodded. A woman whose husband had disappeared in custody – a regiment whose troops she accused of being cannibals and believed they had eaten her husband like they ate dogs and horses – scratched her head. Her scarf was knotted over the scruff behind her head.

'I have consulted our brothers from the Bar. They have suggested we must float an association and fight together as a group. What do you think?' Haleema asked everyone.

'Yes, yes!' the relatives responded.

A gaunt old man, wearing an unkempt waistcoat over a doubled sweater, listened keenly. His face had hardened in attention, and he adjusted his hearing aid keenly to hear Haleema speak. He raised his bony hand to agree.

'Right then,' Haleema said, 'the Bar people have chosen a name for this union of ours. Shall I read it to you…?' She adjusted the belt once more.

The gathering nodded in unison. The young woman with the chocolate-greedy child wiped the snot off her child's nose with her *pheran*'s cuff.

'They want to call it the "Association of Relatives of the Disappeared Persons" – is that okay?' Haleema read, fumbling with the English words she had repeatedly revised to enunciate them properly.

'*Bilkul*! Absolutely!'

'Okay. Now you have to choose the head or president of this association of ours. So decide…' She walked off and sat in the middle of the gathering.

Murmured consultations followed among those sitting. A while later, the old man with the hearing aid spoke loudly in a papery voice, 'I think our head should be Haleema. We are unlettered. She is a bit more experienced than us and she has taken a step like this.'

Everyone agreed. Haleema was confused. She didn't know how to respond to the decision. She hesitated, but it occurred to her that her indecision would be unnatural. She agreed.

'Now we have to register ourselves,' she said after a while, 'so we have to make a list of our names and fill in our particulars and hand it over to the Bar.'

'At once,' the gathering said in one voice.

They all marched to the Bar room.

Advocate Farooq Ahmad was carefully selecting and arranging brick-thick books of law in the High Court library. His silken crow-black gown swept the floor behind him as he walked. He slipped his pince-nez a bit lower and sat in a chair at a long conference table. His legs disappeared beneath the table.

'So, what have you decided?' he asked Haleema, once he saw her enter the library with the relatives, not lifting his head from the book in his hands.

'We have agreed,' all said in chorus, Haleema's voice distinct.

'Very good. Shall we make a list and begin some formalities?'

'Yes, *janaab*.'

Farooq pulled out a long cascade-green sheet of judicial paper from a folder lying next to the stack of books, padded the paper on the folder and used one of the books over a margin as a ruler. He drew three straight rules on the paper, dividing it neatly into five narrow and long columns. On top he wrote: 'List of Members of the Association of the Relatives of the Disappeared Persons'. One by one, he filled the columns:

S No.	Name of the relative	Address	Relation with the missing	Missing relative's name
I.	Raja Begum	Rajwar, Kupwara	Half Widow	Altaf
2.	Muhammad Yaqoob	Rangar Stop, Khanyar	Father	Mushtaq
3.	Sakeena Akhtar	Zero Bridge, Srinagar	Half Widow	Manzoor
4.	Mohammad Ismail	Tangmarg	Son	G. Nabi

And the list continued…

Haleema leaned over the paper as Advocate Farooq called out her name loudly. She took off her spectacles; its steel wire-bridge was wound in thread to keep the hard, blunt metal from sinking in her nose. She wiped the glasses – cutting small D's at their bottoms – with the edge of her voile headgear and put it back on to read the names.

'Since we don't know the status of your respective relatives who have disappeared…we don't know whether they are alive or not…we cannot describe you as widows, or whatever the case may be. We are talking legal language here, and the status matters. So, for all such uncertain cases for women whose husbands have disappeared, we will prefix their status with "Half",' Advocate Farooq explained.

Half. The word ringed in Haleema's head. A cold pinch.

'And what about mothers, Farooq sahib?' Haleema asked. 'Are they half mothers by rule?'

Everyone turned to her. Silence. Advocate Farooq stopped writing and looked over his pince-nez. Whether their children were dead or alive or missing, mothers would remain mothers – but Advocate Farooq was not sure. He didn't know how to respond to Haleema. He couldn't be certain what status of victimhood should be attested to her.

'So am I a half mother?' Haleema repeated.

15

At the wedding

The first thing that the Association of Relatives of the Disappeared Persons decided was to meet Dr Aiyaash Mir, the chief minister. Mir had just come back to power as head of the state after a gap of eight years from a face-saving exile. All ARDP members met in the High Court and sat around in a ring in the park. They had brought with themselves old and worn pictures of their missing sons, husbands and brothers, photographs that had been exhibited excessively. Haleema asked everyone to put the pictures in the centre of the ring. She stood up, squatted in the centre and collected all of them into a wrinkled plastic bag.

They then chose two members to accompany Haleema to Mir: Muhammad Yaqoob, the old man with the hearing aid, and Sakeena, the young woman with a child.

One hazy winter morning, the three went to Izhar.

The same orderly who was there the first time Haleema came to visit Izhar opened the door, first a little, and when he recognized Haleema, wider. He welcomed them in, bolted the door behind their backs, and took them straight to Izhar's house.

The drawing room in Izhar's office-cum-home was clean and simple. A sofa sat squarely on one side and an intricate *namda*, a woollen carpet with coloured yarn work, on the other. A velvet-encased Quran lay on an X-shaped, polished wooden rack on the ledge of a window. Next to the Quran sat a white telephone, and next to it a folded prayer rug.

They sat on the *namda*.

Izhar emerged fresh from his bathroom. His hair was wet and slicked backwards, making him look different, slightly younger.

'We have come with a request,' said Haleema.

'Yes, please go ahead,' Izhar said.

'You have done so much…'

'Don't mention it, please. Go ahead. What do you want me to do?' Izhar interrupted.

'May Allah keep you safe! We want to meet the CM and give him a memorandum. We have come to seek your advice on how to get an appointment.'

'He is outside the state these days. I spoke to the personal secretary of his chief secretary's secretary regarding a news item this morning. I wanted Mir's comment on the excesses of the state task force. But I was told he is out of station.'

'What do we do then?'

'Don't worry. I can arrange your meeting through this secretary. He will in turn arrange it for you with Mir. He knows when he returns. Just a second…'

Izhar lifted the phone and dialed a number. 'Hello!' he spoke into it, '*Assalaam-u-Alaiqum*! I am fine, fine... Actually, some people want to see him… It is very important… Tell me exactly when they can? No. No. They are three only… Hello? Hello?' The line snapped. He redialled. 'Yes…yes… They are only three... Okay!'

He put down the phone. 'I have talked to him. He will do it. You can go to his office today. He will fix and facilitate a meeting,' Izhar assured them.

The orderly brought in cups of *nuun chai* on a large tray with hot crispy *tsotchwaers*, bagels kissed with sesame seeds.

Mir's palatial house was at the foothills of the Zabarwan, the same Zabarwan that overlooked Papa 2. The entrance to the outhouse residency office of the secretary had a multi-tier security layer. Bunkers and check posts were followed by two sliding spiky barricades and coils of razor wire. As Haleema, Sakeena and Yaqoob approached the gate, the guard from a bunker whistled. A slit opened in the gate like that of a letterbox. A pair of unreadable eyes appeared in the slit and looked at them from top to bottom, then right to left. 'What do you want?' a voice asked.

Before Haleema and Sakeena could respond, another voice from the inside called aloud, 'Let them in!' It was the man they had come to see, the personal secretary to the chief secretary's secretary.

The bolts clanked. The gate opened. The pair of eyes became a trooper. Eyes that now seemed unsuited to his face, now that they had an expression. A crude one. Or callous.

The trooper unhooked the coil of the razor wire and slid the barricades aside.

'Come in,' he barked at them.

There were two more checkpoints inside, one at the entrance of the outhouse and another adjacent to it, with a dirty green curtain for the ladies.

A lady trooper frisked the two women while continuing to chat with the trooper who had opened the gate. Her hair was excessively oiled and tightly gathered into a bun. A smudged dot of vermilion displayed itself proudly from her forehead. Her hands were rough, dry and grubby. She frisked Haleema and Sakeena thoroughly before letting them in.

Further inside, in what looked like a plush solarium, a pot-bellied man in a dark brown suit awaited them. A brooch exhibited itself prominently from his jacket's lapel, an enamelled red miniature ploughshare plated on a chip of metal. He had dyed his hair black recently; traces of the dye remained on the edges of his grizzled sideburns where the mirror had deceived him. His incisors stood out and fell onto his lower lip. They needed bracing.

He sat them on a sofa and then sunk himself in one across them. Though the room was warm from an already extinguished tin brazier, the mottled green marmoreal floor was stinging cold.

'See, I cannot say no to Izhar despite being extremely busy,' he said. 'Actually, Mir sahib doesn't meet anybody. Neither here at home nor at the secretariat. He is very busy these days. Very, very busy. So he cannot meet you here or there. I am sorry. But since you are Izhar's friends, I must help you. Mir sahib will arrive from Delhi tomorrow and he won't see anyone. But he is invited to my daughter's wedding the day after tomorrow, at Zakura. You can come there. I will arrange a meeting there, if not a long one, at least a short one. Is that okay?' he asked.

'Sure. That is most excellent,' said Haleema. Sakeena and Yaqoob nodded.

'Okay, see you there then.'

The secretary tore off a strip of paper from the edge of an Urdu newspaper lying on a glass table in front of him, and wrote an address on it. Then he gave the paper to Haleema. 'Here. This is my address,' he said.

Haleema showed the piece of paper to a Zakura grocer and asked him for directions to the secretary's house. 'Go straight and turn where the road turns right,' the grocer told her.

The road began to resemble a militarized zone the closer they got to the house. Lines and arrows were drawn in chalk on the road to guide the very important persons and the very very important persons. All the guests were frisked. So were they. The house was cloistered with lights, an intermittent flicker of yellow, green, red and blue. A large marquee in the courtyard was full of chattering women. Clouds of smoke rose up from beside the marquee. A *wur*, an open kitchen, had been arranged where the *waazwaan*, the traditional Kashmiri wedding banquet, was being cooked by a team of *waazaas*, chefs. A few women wearing heavy jewellery and make-up crossed the lawn between the house and the marquee, leaving behind the scent of their cheap perfumes in the air.

Haleema, Sakeena and Yaqoob looked like uninvited strangers or beggars in this festive, upper-class atmosphere. Kashmir, it seemed to them, had forgotten to celebrate weddings in this manner; only those who could afford the security could celebrate it to the fullest.

The three hesitated to ask anyone about the secretary and slowly walked towards the *wur* where some men sat in red plastic chairs, talking about politics, chuckling and watching over the *waazwaan*. A *waazaa* in a shroud-like soup-and-soot-stained *pheran* squatted in front of a platter placed on a bed of glowing embers. The platter was full of lamb chops. His right hand was swathed in a dirty rag, which he unrolled and rolled around the hand over and over again.

More *waazaas* sat on reedmats behind thick slabs of slippery stones. They were beating flat the already beaten dollops of pink lamb salamis with large wooden hammers. Battered, the dollops thinned in the centre and thickened on the edges like blown-out bubbles of chewing gum. The sounds of their disconcerted strikes filled the *wur*. With each thud, Haleema mysteriously felt a certain sense of loss, a loss of time or something else. It made her heart palpitate. She could not look at the variety of lamb dishes, which were being readied in enormous round vessels over hefty burning cinders and logs. A young boy was volunteering with a *samovar* of saffron kahwa, his pants' legs rolled up. Like a tender at a tavern, he poured kahwa into small cups for the *waazaas*. With each cup he handed out a *bakirkhaani* from a lidded willow basket.

The aroma of the food around them watered their mouths, but the three felt unwelcome. The boy offered them kahwa but Haleema politely refused. 'No, thank you,' she said. A man from the *wur* rose and walked towards them. 'Yes. What do you want?' he asked Haleema.

'We are looking for Secretary sahib. He knows us,' said Haleema humbly.

'Secretary sahib called *you*?' he said, puzzled, screening them from top to bottom.

After a pause, he said, 'Okay, come with me.'

He led them to the front verandah of the house and sat them in wicker chairs. 'Wait here. I shall call him for you,' he said and went inside the house.

A row of *tumbaknaers* stood along a large window facing the verandah. The granite floor was strewn with toffee wrappers.

The door to the corridor inside was open, and the smell of *isband*, Syrian rue-seeds, and a blend of fragrances wafted out. Some giggling and whispering teenage girls passed in and out of the house in pairs. They wore gaudy make-up and fancy dresses. Three children fought over a toffee with another. The fourth threw it on the floor to get rid of the nuisance. The other three ravenously pounced on the discarded sweet and fought amongst themselves further. Done with the sweet, they pursued the *madrigals* of singing women, mimicking them and then guffawing. A chubby woman with heavy make-up sprinkled rue-seeds on a smoking *isband-soz*. A new cloud of fragrant smoke added further mystique to the ceremonial ambience.

The secretary finally showed up, looking constipated, least expecting Haleema and her companions to turn up. He had forgotten his invitation and now despised their presence. But he couldn't avoid them. He regarded them coldly as if they had spoiled the fervour of the wedding. 'Oh you all! So you are here,' he said, suppressing a yawn.

'Wait here till Mir sahib arrives,' he told them.

They nodded gratefully.

After some more waiting, a whistle from a distant siren suddenly pricked the air. Aiyaash Mir had finally arrived. All the men rushed to the gate to receive him, expressing more enthusiasm for Mir than for the bridegroom. An arched white tent had mysteriously erected a tunnel over the lane, while the red carpet below was ready to welcome him.

The siren stopped; the first footsteps to dirty the carpet were of the carbine-wielding commandos escorting Mir. The commandos looked hither and thither, and finally Mir emerged from the confines of his vehicle. He donned a grey tricot *pheran* and a black *karakuli* and wore dark sunglasses even at that late hour. He was followed by ministers and bureaucrats dressed in grey safari suits.

Mir was directly ushered to the drawing room, and everybody hankered after him. 'You wait here unless called,' the secretary told the three of them, shoving them back into the chairs as they tried to follow him too.

The trio overheard felicitations and congratulations being exchanged inside, then once all the exchanges were done, the talk inside the house dropped to a murmur.

A few minutes later, the door to the corridor opened and they were called in. The commando guarding the door of the drawing room frisked Yaqoob and the plastic bag that Haleema carried. They stoked through the pictures of the missing, the newspaper clippings and the papers of their petitions.

The drawing room where Mir sat had an Iranian carpet and matching tinselwork cushions. The windows had heavy crewel curtains with suitable pelmets. The room smelt of newly bought clothes.

There was no place for them to sit save in front of the doorway. When they finally sat down, everyone except the secretary went to another room. Mir sat sideways, reclining against a low round cushion. A porcelain plate from which he had eaten lay on a floral, transparent plastic tablecloth in front of him. The remains of a half-eaten kebab and a whole fried chicken wing stared vacantly from the plate. Mir stretched out one leg and folded the other under him. His *karakuli* was a little tilted now. Before Haleema or Sakeena or Yaqoob could say anything, he began to speak. 'I know all your stories. Secretary sahib has briefed me. Tell me what I can do?' he said in a voice as if he were sharing a secret. His jowls shook as he uttered the words.

'*Janaab*, we need your help to trace our relatives,' Yaqoob said.

'The culprits must be brought to the court to at least admit what they did to our loved ones,' said Sakeena.

'We must have justice,' said Haleema.

Mir took a long pause before responding.

'What if I say that many of those who you think are missing have crossed the border and will never come back? How can we bring them back? How is the state responsible for them?'

'Our loved ones were picked up in front of us, *janaab*. Our neighbours saw them being taken away,' said Haleema, genially. 'And no relative – no father, mother, wife, anyone – would drag themselves to the media, to the courts, the police, the army camps, jails, mortuaries for so long to search for their loved ones if they had done that – crossed the border. No one would have gone mad among us if that were the case. We've become beggars, as you can see. Had they been killed by the army in front of us, we would have stayed put and silent throughout our lives, and with no expectations, no hopes, and no despair. But this longing is a pain. An eternal torture. It has not abated for a second. It kills us every day and resurrects us every morning to kill us again. Please feel for us.'

Haleema and Sakeena sobbed. Mir regarded them sharply.

'I have gone through the same madness myself,' he said. 'My wife is in America. My son is in America. My daughters are here and there. My family is scattered. I am here. I keep no trace of my family. I am like you. Actually we are all the same. We can't do anything. I can just pray for you.'

Mir stood up immediately and in no time his men assembled around him. He was ready to leave now.

The siren began to ring once again.

16

Alternatives

Army camps, torture centres, police stations, jails, wetlands and mortuaries had been searched. Social leaders, journalists, politicians, bureaucrats, NGOs and courts had been approached. Clues after clues had been traded but the truth remained lost in the shadow of war. Finally, in the summer of 1999, Justice Aadil Khan concluded the long inquiry and summoned the army. For once, Haleema was thrilled, for it was the day she thought she would finally know what happened to Imran.

She sat in a plastic-and-steel fitment in the court's lobby with Advocate Farooq. The lobby's semi-transparent fibreglass roof allowed the sun to seep through warmly. The stairs and corridors were filled with black-robed lawyers and their frustrated clients.

A colonel entered the lobby, guarded by four carbine-wielding men in camouflage olives. He wore an olive Stetson with a strap that ran under his clean-shaved double-chin. Even in the heat of June he donned a high-neck silken army scarf. A name screamed from the badge on his pocket: Col. Ajit Kumar. He held a brown folder under his arm. He stopped in the middle of the lobby and looked around. Then he strolled towards the fitment and halted. 'You would be Haleema, right?' he asked.

Haleema gazed at him and shook her head.

'And you would be representing the army, right?' Advocate Farooq responded.

'Right, Mister…?' he asked, offering his hand, smiling.

Advocate Farooq shook his hand and glanced at the folder.

'So what does the army want?' he asked.

'Peace,' said the colonel.

'Or pacification?' Farooq retorted.

'Perhaps. Pacification is the first cousin of peace.'

Haleema didn't understand anything from their conversation in English except the word 'peace'. She had heard the word several times now. And each time she heard it, it stimulated an imagination of a desolate street patrolled by troops on a cloudy day.

'There seem to be no dearth of alternatives for the likes of you. Despite the alternatives, the meaning fades away ultimately, and words become hollow shells of a nut, illusively pieced together, giving an impression of the kernel inside,' Farooq said.

'Alternatives. That is a word you have uttered. I would stop at that word, before going into meaninglessness. In the end, we all have to cope with alternatives,' the colonel maintained.

'Were it possible for alternatives to replace justice, we would have been lucky in the world. Imagine all of us, settling our scores by employing alternatives, without messing anything up. But I am afraid it is not.'

The colonel leaned forward and turned to Haleema before lowering his voice. 'In plain words…it is not wise to dig up the past. It won't yield anything. Let us start a new beginning from today. We can't bring you your culprits. But I personally feel a moral responsibility towards healing your wounds, Haleema. I am not talking about any compensation. Never. But I feel I should take care of you for the rest of your life. And fulfil your wishes, if any, in my power. We can begin with a monetary help of two lakhs. If you need more, if you wish…you must not hesitate,' the colonel told Haleema.

Haleema smiled her private smile, but this time publicly. Farooq watched quietly, intrigued, not interceding.

'I won't live longer than the money I have saved. And what would I do with the money you are offering me? Would it assuage my pain? No. I don't want any justice from you. Not really. You are incapable of justice. If you honestly want to help me, tell me what happened to my son? What did they, I mean Major Aman Kushwaha, do with him? Is my son alive or…' She broke down.

'I wish I could tell you,' said the colonel.

Advocate Farooq's personal assistant, a tall and thin man with a bundle of files under his arm, arrived to inform them that Justice Aadil Khan had left on an emergency and wouldn't be available for any hearing that day.

The colonel unstrapped his hat, put it under his free arm, took some steps towards the exit to leave but stopped, walked back towards Haleema and muttered to her, 'The least I can tell you is this: Major Aman Lal Kushwaha was killed long ago in an attack on the border.'

Haleema felt sad. Kushwaha was her one and only hope for Imran's whereabouts. She was stunned at hearing the news, but not relieved. She grieved at the fact that he had been the only one who could tell her what happened to Imran, and now, with the news of his death, she was half-certain about Imran too. Her heart pounded heavily. She felt weak in her knees; her legs began to fail her. She became oblivious of her presence in the noisy and crowded market outside the High Court but she strutted on mechanically. She didn't even know that she had begun to weep, and everyone she passed by was awfully staring at her. *Imu is not alive*, her heart was telling her.

I have to keep hoping, she murmured to herself minutes later. *I cannot be defeated like this. I cannot lose him like this.* She wiped her tears, corrected her dupatta and pulled herself together. *I have to go home and keep waiting. Yes. That is the only thing I have to do.*

17

Appearances and disappearances

The battered hope inside her was still alive.

A part of Haleema still believed Imran would return, even as she sat motionless in the kitchen, repeatedly rubbing her gnarled hands over the vapour-smothered window, staring at the wooden gate, wailing under her breath, sharpening her gaze every now and then.

In the distance, a few children shone their torchlights into the night sky, the intersecting beams dancing gracefully against the morose darkness.

She sat there until the birds, flock after flock, returned to their nests. Until the bats rose from their roost and began to flit this way and that, crashing into walls and windowpanes. Until the clamour of distant, almost synchronized, shutters rolled down. Until the pandemonium of traffic began to fade away. Until intangible ghostly shapes became vivid and came alive as threads and knots of darkness. Until a scarred moon began to gleam dimly through a cloudy screen. Until the exclamations, cries, whispers, shouts, thuds and bangs of the world outside halted. She waited and waited and waited...

In my long solitary walks,
sometimes
I have imagined you as
someone,
distant to me,
somewhere,
walking in the middle of a lonely road,
then turning around

only to become
someone else.
Your face blurs,
tiring my eyes.

The night is tired now,
the old moon, hanging in the dark sky,
is tired too,
the roads are tired,
your footprints are tired,
the candle, the windows, the doors are tired–
I am still waiting,
come now…

The barking of dogs filled the darkness. A lone motorcycle throttled loudly, racing up her heart. The siren of an ambulance grew louder and louder, until it reached a crescendo and gradually died out.

The night began to suffuse everything, stifling the furore of the day. The noise from the world outside tuned down to a low babble. She sat through the silent hours, till the silence became a whistle in her ears.

When her leg began to prickle and sore, she stepped out into the cold night, a candle in her hand. She arranged her shoes on the wooden rack on the verandah. She noticed the soles had almost melted away. She then went to inspect the latch on the backyard shack's door and discovered a drenched whimpering puppy playing with an old shoe of hers in the pool of candlelight, while a swollen sparrow cowered amid a stack of faggots. She left the door open and returned to the verandah, spreading a blue tarpaulin over the damp sawdust that had been left to dry for the winter's *kaangers*. She left the candle on the edge of the verandah and ambled over to the gate to bolt it, but she paused there for a while, in some vague expectation, and returned, leaving it unlocked.

Before slipping under her quilt, she popped nearly half a dozen peach- and white-coloured pills and capsules. The glasses and the pair of fake gold earrings were removed carefully. The candle was blown out, the smoking, aglow wick snuffed out with a pinch, before she slipped into her bed to try and get some sleep.

Outside, the night remained awake.

She was awoken by a sharp knock on the door in the middle of the night. Haleema got up immediately, sweating. Her heart hammered within her chest. The electricity had returned. She switched on the dim corridor lights and huffed towards the door, staggering. She opened the door and saw a boy sitting outside, shivering, through the netted door. Her hands trembled as she unbolted it. The boy wore an army hat and carried something under his arm. She switched on the bulb of the verandah but it didn't work – she had forgotten that it had fused a long time ago. As the figure walked closer, she was shocked to find the boy was Imran. Her throat dried up at once. Her jaw hung loose.

No questions were asked and no answers were given. Haleema remained frozen for a long while, her eyes not blinking at all. She didn't know what to say. Imran thrust himself close to her and hugged her for a long time. Haleema's hands didn't respond to his hug. She felt almost faint.

'Don't ask anything,' Imran whispered. 'Nothing.'

Haleema wept uncontrollably, silently.

'Don't ask where I have been,' Imran said. 'I need to fix the chinstrap of my hat. It snapped at one end,' he pointed towards his right ear. 'Then I want to put my head in your lap and sleep for some time. I am so tired. So tired. I have been running and running all this time.'

He then placed his head on his mother's lap. Haleema's cheeks stilled.

'What is in this file?' she asked him.

'Records of all the places I have been to,' he said.

Her tears didn't stop. She stroked his dusty hair till he fell asleep.

After some time she too fell asleep and began to dream:

It is Eid, about the time when Imran is just five years old. They are sitting in the vast lawns of Hazratbal mosque. Haleema is in the middle of a congregational Eid prayer amidst a sea of women, while Imran tries to escape; Haleema clutches his wrist to not let him go.

Yet, in a fraction of a second, he manages to slip out of her grip. Haleema waits till the prayers have ended, believing he is somewhere nearby. But he isn't. He is nowhere to be found. She stands up now and turns around, scanning the gathering as far as she can, as far as her eyes can see.

A white-turbaned man in an embroidered grey tunic appears with his assistant under the dome. The women raise their hands and beseech him to bless them. Each pair of eyes struggles to catch a glimpse of the holy relic in the man's right hand. Yet Haleema is the only one who doesn't care for him. Some women look oddly at her. Some construe from her evident panic that something has happened to her. She stares at the last row, where some beggars sit cross-legged. She cannot find him. She stands paralysed with worry and fear.

A while later, she finds herself jostling through a crowd in the market outside the mosque, nudging her way through a crawling, market-probing, window-shopping, bargaining crowd of people. She walks past the shops selling earthen pitchers and willow bats; past the showrooms that display prayer rugs with flossed tassels; past all the parantha and *monj goel* sellers; past the women who sell lotus seeds; past the barefooted filthy man who sells masala from a cart. She approaches a small tent at the end where a group of volunteers take down details of missing people. A large table sits beside the volunteers with a megaphone on it. Some men sit behind the table, and one of them is the Imam of Natipora. Haleema wonders what he is doing there.

A fleeting moment later, she realizes she is not in Hazratbal but in front of a desk outside the shrine in Natipora. She is crying and trying to tell the men sitting at the missing persons' tent that her son has been picked up by the army. Suddenly, she can no longer speak. She attempts a scream. But the louder she screams, the hollower, more muted she feels.

Again, there was a sudden knock on the door.

Haleema woke up with a jerk, realizing she was crying in her sleep. The sun-lit gaps between the curtains told her it was already late morning. Before Haleema could pull herself together to realize what she had just dreamt, the knock grew louder and harder. She staggered to the door and unbolted it. She found Sakeena on the verandah.

'What happened to you? I have been knocking for a long time now. Is everything all right?' Sakeena asked, worried, as Haleema opened the door to let her in.

Haleema sighed and said, 'Yes, everything is all right. I just slept a bit longer.'

'Okay. But since we have to attend the protest meet at Pratap Park today…' Sakeena reminded her.

'Yes. Yes. I remember. I am sorry. Has everyone already assembled?'

'Yes, but not in the park. The police didn't allow us. We are all scattered about Lal Chowk.'

'Why? Why didn't the police allow them?'

'The government is filling the park with a new layer of soil and sowing new turf into it. There is no place for us to sit in the park now,' Sakeena said.

Book III

Random Notes

by Izhar

The clock on the wall tells me you are late. Razaaq brings me yesterday's tough, stale, sesame-seed-smothered bagels with a cup of *nuun chai*. He tells me fetching *tsot* from the baker these days is almost the same as committing suicide – it's so cold, he will freeze at the crossroad and become a statue, like a snowman.

So, I manage.

I am worried about Haleema. Any stray thought of her, kind of, scares me. She can hardly move now. Her back has failed her. She told me the other day that she had to crawl up to her bathroom. I had a lump in my throat when she said this. Her eyesight too is betraying her. I got her strips and strips of pills and tubes of gels yesterday. But I know medicines aren't enough. What she needs is company.

Years have gone by in vain…

Rain has ruined ARDP's protest programme at Pratap Park. The relatives take shelter under the dripping awning of a newspaper office's tin roof. Their white headbands and armbands, with featureless faces painted on them, are still tied around their appendages. They look injured, in every way.

I slip my voice recorder back into my jacket and call them inside, to the lawn of my office building. Haleema is with them. It's good to see she has convalesced a little. Her shoulders are still hunched, perhaps because of the cold. She sits on the bottom of the steps that lead to the entrance of my office. As she cleans her wire-rimmed glasses with the corner of her scarf, I realize that she looks delusively bland without them, a demure person, not herself. The glasses have left behind two bean-shaped impressions on her nose.

The rain thins to an intermittent spray. The smell of earth wafts about the lawn.

I call my colleagues from the local media to speak to the relatives. Soul by strolling soul, they walk in with their notepads and cameras. I go out back, over to the lawn, and see that some of them have already begun training their cameras. Haleema has unfolded an old newspaper on a dry stair, and her companions toss photographs of their loved ones on it.

I see some children too, waiting, with placards cut out of cardboard cartons and searing words written with black markers: 'Where is my father?' More than eight thousand are missing in Kashmir today. This truth is hard for the government to dismiss easily, or swallow as such.

Haleema stands, and, supporting her back with her hand, speaks fiercely to the gathering. Everybody looks at her intently, and nods agreeably. Where could they have possibly gone, the missing relatives, the loved ones?

When all eventually return once the protest is over, she stays back, and we chat. 'I am not struggling for my son now but for all those who have disappeared,' she tells me passionately. This is her life now.

I smell a roasting stench coming from her. Our eyes roll around. She takes out her *kaanger* from under her pheran and holds it aloft, almost level to her eyes. Its wooden *tsalan*, the stoker, is half extinguished. What remains is a glowing angry ember suspended on a grimy white thread. The smoke makes her scowl. She frantically brings out the smoking end and, bearing the heat between her fingers, throws it on the lawn. 'They don't leave us, these *kaangers*,' she says, smiling. 'I'd forgotten it was inside the pheran.'

It scares me – that she would forget. Another lapse of memory when she is home alone and God knows what could happen.

I ask her whether she has money to go home. She nods. I still force a folded banknote into her palm. She averts my fist. The note gets crumpled in the ensuing bickering. I finally thrust it into a side pocket of her pheran.

I spend the rest of the day dusting my small library, smoothing the ends and corners of dog eared volumes. I find my frequently used references have gone missing. I haven't kept a count of who I have lent them to. And why. *Jonathan Livingston Seagull, Animal Farm, Wuthering Heights, The Death of Ivan Ilyich* – everything that shaped my understanding of the world. Then I notice more titles are missing, taken by friends and acquaintances and never returned: *One Hundred Years of Solitude, The Stranger, Waiting for Godot, Spartacus, Crime and Punishment,* some Shakespeare, Chekhov, Maupassant, and some others I don't even remember.

I pick out *The Waste Land* from in between volumes of spiral-bound reports on international conflicts. The reports on Kashmir are on the lower shelves – handy, yet dusty, scrabbled and shop-soiled. Kashmir is mentioned everywhere – in books, news reports, political reports – but it has disappeared from the world, an enforced disappearance of its own.

Got a call about an encounter in Chadoora; have to go cover it.

The car's cold engine doesn't start. Instead, it screeches redundantly. I try harder, repeatedly, synchronizing the accelerator with each turn of the key. Razaaq watches wide-eyed until his gaze meets mine. He funnily bats his eyelids in embarrassment and then rushes inside.

He brings out a jug of tepid water and pours it over the windscreen. The warm water swiftly travels to the bonnet, leaving vapour in its trail. I open the bonnet and pour the remaining water on the engine. The car finally begins to show some life but dies on me once more. One more try later, it begins to roar.

The car is an old model and bought second-hand; a stubborn old fool that obliges me reluctantly during chilly winters. But once it begins to chug, it doesn't betray me.

I pick the wrong way to travel. I take the parabolic bridge of Amira Kadal, but I should have chosen Budshah Kadal instead. A traffic jam crams the whole bridge. As I snail up, angry with my decision to choose this bridge, I see a row of fisherwomen seated on the ashlar-lined kerb with tubs full of fish, some swimming, others dead on their sides. Jigar Maas, the old, heavy silver-wearing fisherwoman sits on one edge, bickering and bargaining with some customers from the army. The car is sluggishly waltzing behind a bus. I begin to honk desperately, incessantly. I find a gap and squeeze through.

I arrive in Chadoora around noon and park the car near an apple orchard, where I see that a few of my colleagues have already arrived. I take a detour off the dirt road, taking a shortcut through a paddy field. I trudge along the hedgerows carefully. A distant wail grows louder with each step closer to the site of the encounter.

There's a smell of something burning in the air. I climb a swampy strip of land and startle some roosting ducks. My feet become heavier with the mud sticking to the soles. From up here, I can now see thick grey mushrooms of smoke swirling up; the whole village has been burned down to smoke out a single militant. Around thirty houses have been destroyed, consumed by the fire. Was it a reprimand for sympathizing with dissenters? Or was it a 'psy-op' – psychological operation? Perhaps. I can't see any other press personnel. I suppose they have all gone to the police station, where the body of the militant has been taken.

The remains of the day: craters, jagged edges of gutted walls, brick detritus, crashed fences, charred rice, ashen straw, gaunt remnants of a mangled bicycle, oddments of cloth, shattered glass, roasted poultry; mooing, burnt cows, dancing in pain. Some men have begun sorting out reusable wood from the cindered ones. Amid all the wails and sobs, some women clear out the scorched grain with winnow-pans from the lentil in their barns. Some hunker over the debris, while one chews the hem of her dupatta.

I am surprised to find I am one of the first journalists to reach the spot; I don't know what to do. How odd, how odd it feels to be reporting from places like these. To stand around and keep asking the stupidest questions, and not being able to help. How odd!

I strike a conversation with the men. They are quick to gather who I am. One of them clears a large dusty boulder with the sleeve of his pheran and beckons me to sit on it. A very respectful gesture. I bring out the notepad and note down what they have to say. A bulge runs down the middle of the pad, its corners soggy, creased and ragged. The thing looks depressed.

I cease to feel who I am. What am I doing here? I feel like a joker in a solemn audience. When I start recording their laments, I am at the risk of being countered by the overwhelming nature of their reports – I cannot think this way…I cannot…

Spring turns a hard, brisk winter into a soft, rainy March. I have two things to do today:

a) Attend a press conference by the army
b) Attend to an invitation by Haleema, to lay the foundation stone for a memorial for the missing people of Kashmir.

That is.

I enter the cantonment area in Sonwar on a foggy morning. A dull sun struggles to shine from behind grey clouds. The road slithers through gun barrels, coils of razor-wire and evenly placed stones that slow down my car. An elaborate signboard overhead tells me 'Welcome to Badami Bagh Cantonment'.

Welcome indeed!

The colonel sits across a large, carved walnut-wood desk, bracketed between his subordinates, and checks with his long fingers the alignment of his striped blue and red scarf against his drooping jowls.

He checks his panel of multi-coloured medal ribbons, reassures himself of his service stripes and dusts his epaulettes. He turns towards a subordinate to ask him if he, the colonel, looks fine.

The room bombilates with the chatter of reporters while their cameras are ready to go.

Between the media and the colonel's desk lies a table upholstered in white, with a decorated cache of arsenal surrendered by men who the colonel links with Al Fatah – a militant outfit, according to my memory, long self-dissolved. The army has written the name of their battalion with bullets, arranged in order on the table to make it read 'C-117-RR'. LMG bullets hyphenate the battalion's bullet display.

The surrendered militants enter the room just before the colonel clears his throat to speak. They are all tall and almost the same height. They wear scarves and only the glint of light from their eyes can be seen. There are five empty chairs in front of the table, facing us, where the militants sit for our perusal. They wear frazzled, faded sleeveless sweaters over warm Pathan suits.

'Do you think our press conferences are mere PR exercises? The truth will reveal itself to you today. I give you these men without my intervention. They will tell you why they surrendered. Over to you!' The colonel brags confidently and rises to get off the high table. He stops and turns to add, 'And yes, today is a special day, a day of redemption, and we are not letting you go without tea and snacks... No! Hot kebabs are waiting outside.' He thumps the table and leaves with the note of treat.

I can tell you how many mouths began to water with this announcement.

The reporters gear up and thrust microphones into the faces of the masked men, who speak an unmistakable dialect from the south-west, which means they are no militants. That area does not belong to militants.

I leave with a wry smile to fulfil my next appointment, and go back to Press Enclave to fetch my digicam. I am hampered by protesters inside the enclave. I park the car outside and walk through them. I am neither interested nor intrigued by these protestors. This is a daily business. A stale routine. They are here everyday: unemployed doctors, wageless transporters, victims of police extortion, people without electricity in their homes (or people with electricity once a week, or worse, twice a month), people without water in their taps, people without roads in their villages, people without hospitals for their sick, price hike protestors, ad-hoc government servants, disowned Unani doctors...the list goes on.

Not far from where the Mazaar-e-Shohda, the Martyrs' Graveyard, is, relatives of the disappeared are busy demarcating an area to build a memorial for the vanished. I gaze over the silent bulges and plaques, try to read rain-washed, wind-eroded, half-erased and smudged names and dates on the flinty epitaphs. A gentle breeze blows from north to south. Some of my colleagues who have resisted the army's offer of kebabs and have even suffered censorship and threats have already reached ahead of me. Some more reporters from the press conference have also arrived, bits of army meat still stuck in their teeth. I can confidently vouch for their tongues frolicking within their mouths, trying to pick their teeth. I can picture them now, with bone-china army plates and their conversations over kebabs that hide their capricious subconscious. Journalism was once the other name of resistance. So much has changed. So much.

Haleema sits on a grassy mound at a distance from the men. She is dreamily pensive, embracing a slippery black marble plaque against the side of her leg, as if she has been sitting on a riverbank.

'*Assalaam-u-Alaiqum*!' In wishing her, I jerk her out of her trance. Her face twitches first and then breaks into a smile. 'How are you?' she asks. Her dupatta waves and flutters in the gale, revealing the salt-and-pepper in her hair. She draws the dupatta back over and points at the plaque.

It is beautiful, I remark.

She wipes the shiny surface with her hand. 'Isn't it?'

A young boy demands to see the plaque; Haleema hands it to him. A mason has constructed a cenotaphic block of bricks and left an impression on its front to fix the plaque in. There are remains of fresh mortar around the bricks.

The mason, a man in grey Pathan coat and wearing a white, conical Kashmiri cap, is chiselling out clean lines in the cement, abutting the bricks with the edge of his anvil. With each scrape he stops, his face lambent, and he marvels at the perfection of his abrasions.

'Come,' Haleema tells me, following the young boy who proudly holds the plaque now.

I have barely switched on my camera when two rusty and battered police jeeps sashay towards the vast graveyard. The men in the back of the jeeps get off even before the vehicles come to a complete halt and come prowling towards the gathering. They wield short assault rifles and grunt out their breaths. Their pants are stuffed inside their thick jute-brown socks. The officer-in-charge wears a brown leather jacket, suiting his chubby cheeks and the toothbrush moustache – not unlike Hitler's.

They collectively pounce on men and women alike. They shoo Haleema away. I intervene. The officer tells me not to. 'Stay away, we are here to restore law and order.' I still insist.

'Don't meddle, is that clear?'

I don't budge and get dragged away like everybody else. The police were once passionate about safeguarding Kashmiris. Hundreds of them had taken to the streets to avenge the death of their colleague by the army. They had seized the control room in Srinagar, fortified it with arms and boomed '*Hum Kya Chahtay? Azaadi*!' The memory is ironic and brings a wry smile to my lips. Again.

The mason too has been hounded, his sack of tools confiscated. Irate relatives begin holding hands in a ring. Some of the cops aim their rifles at a wider, yet risky, angle to the sky and fire. Everyone ducks, except Haleema.

The officer gestures towards her. I intervene once more. He stops, turns and shouts out his words as a threat, finally: 'Mr Izhar – I said do not meddle. Is that clear?'

I am surprised he knows my name. He knows who I am. I step back and let the police do what they want. I see a situation building up here. I must be quiet for a while and cease to disapprove their actions. The mood of violence must be defused. After all, they have fired warning shots. That is hint enough. What can you do in a place where you can get killed like a stray cat or dog, and be thrown away to rot in the wild?

I tell myself to show some steadfastness. For if I don't – and I know I don't matter – they will take this event for granted. I will use this resolve, this firm conviction – in what I was doing and will do – later. I stand my ground and let them see me, let them see what I stand for.

As the space between me and them widens, I stand where I am, as if tethered to a stake. I witness the last cop, his beard almost touching his eyes, vandalize the cenotaph with a hard kick. I watch him pick up the plaque and walk away with it. I hear faint squalls of protests as the jeeps shut their doors on the bundled relatives and scream off.

The breeze has now become a blustery, howling wind. My shirt flaps and sticks against my chest, like slaps of mercy. I stand alone, watching over the empty spread of Idgah, the dismantled cenotaph and the windblown plastic bags ballooning about in the air.

Less than an hour later, I am at the Safa Kadal police station, in front of the officer, in his room, separated by a thick silence and his voluminous, boastful table, which in no way seems to suit his job and the manner he goes about it. Crude.

That is a part of the larger story of this valley – a veneer. I have seen Gandhi's portraits in torture chambers. Verses of mercy and favour from the Quran on the walls of encounter specialists. So no wonder for me, this.

The officer takes his hat off, revealing a butter-cream tonsure. He pirouettes a glass paperweight on the table and speaks. 'What do you want? Why have you come here?' he asks.

You thought you could ask your men to fire to scare us all and whisk these innocent, doubly victimized people away, and then expect me to go home like a good boy – no. You thought wrong. I am a wet cloth, I will stick to you at all times: This is what I want to tell him.

Release them, I tell him simply, quietly.

'Can't.'

Why not?

'Don't teach me what I should do.'

A long pause.

Our eyes stare into each other, unblinking.

'Okay. I will let the women go for now.'

I don't say anything and give him a solemn nod. I know a further tussle can lead to disappointment.

He presses the bell on his table; a constable enters by default.

'Release the women,' he thunders.

'Yes *janaab*,' the constable replies.

And the children?

A pause, once again.

'And the children,' he adds.

He gives me a sweeping look as I leave his room.

Haleema's house is a moth-eaten structure of wood. The jaded windows are nailed shut, the once-coloured panes now replaced with plain glass. Her courtyard is a jungle of weeds, nettle and bushes, grass growing out of every nook and corner.

I help Haleema out of the car. I am terrified to see her shaking in her fever. She breathes from her mouth and gestures to me to take her straight to her bedroom, where she sleeps on a mattress on the floor. Her breath now sounds like an unoiled see-saw. She sinks directly into bed and props herself up on a pair of pillows, then fumbles into the pockets of her pheran to feel for her inhaler. She puckers on the thing and inhales a succession of fume-like medicine.

Within the reach of her hands is a switch suspended from a red-

and-blue wire that leads to a bulb hanging by a rusty nail from the weary, unpainted teak ceiling. I feel an urge to fetch a tumbler of water. She understands, but is reluctant to be served by me and hesitates as I stand up. I go to the kitchen nevertheless.

The sink is full of unwashed dishes. Crusted brown pieces of rice float at the bottom of a pressure cooker. A wok with tea-imbued strainer, a boiler stained with dried milk on its walls, an odd stack of plates, ladles, spoons, bowls, tureens – all unclean, her reason for her hesitation.

Several knotted plastic bags full of sun-dried vegetables hang by a row of nails from the wooden rafter. I lift the lid off a skillet placed near the stove. There are some collard-greens in it. The aroma of its mixed spices strikes me, forcing me to taste some.

Kitchens are chambers of secrets in one's home, I learn.

I fill a glassful of water into a steel tumbler and take it to Haleema, who readily gulps it down and feigns her wellbeing; it's a signal that I should no longer be held up because of her. That she is absolutely fine, although she can barely conceal her feverish sweaty brow, her tired eyes and shuddering shoulders. To debate her health with her and insist on my moral obligations is to impugn her will. Besides, it is ultimately futile. I pretend to accept her pretensions and leave.

I return to drop Razaaq at her house, with some food and antibiotics. She pallidly smiles at me. I smile back.

Haleema says she has been talking to the walls since ages – perhaps with the cracks and nails too. She tells me they hadn't responded to her for long, but now they do. 'I swear, I swear...they do. They are decisive when I am riddled with doubts... They talk to me...and... and I heed their advice and their compelling counsel... They are my best friends, these walls.'

These days I brood on the idea of gifting her a colour television with cable; rather, not as a gift but planting it right there in her gloomy bedroom. The idea seems weird but is necessary. She might illusively sense someone is with her in the house with the television blaring in the background. Someone who wouldn't complain to shut down at her whim.

But is there anything really worth watching on TV? Though my profession compels me to watch the news at all times, I prefer other matter (you can call it frivolous, if you'd like). I can spend entire weekends glued to Tom and Jerry without a blink. You would laugh, I know. But what else is there to cherish than a small, powerless, impishly tough creature doggedly mocking the big and powerful? The tussle between the two goes on and on. The important thing is that neither of the two die. The interesting fact is, the tussle doesn't end.

'Where are our dear ones?'

A missing person's relative holds aloft a placard with these words at the Srinagar Municipal Park. There are others too, all with white headbands tied on their heads. They mutually console each other. Haleema is there too, holding a picture of Imran. The white margin has the word 'Laapata' scribbled across it: 'missing'. Then there is the small placard planted in the earth that reads: 'We can't forget the past as it is the strength of our future.'

There are two other women here: Parveena and old Mughli, who points and calls me out. As I sit, touching one knee with the ground and the other hunched, in front of her, she touches my face with the flat of her hand with a smile and then kisses my touch on her palm, blessing me. '*Muujood thavinai*, May God keep you.'

All of them know me now. I might be a sinner but I have their blessings. This makes me happy, as happy as blue skies can make one feel. As soon as all the relatives assemble, a contingent of police arrives in the park, crushing their way through dried chinar leaves strewn over and along a footway. They hit and stab the ground with their long bamboo sticks as they walk in, their chest guards worn like squarish cardboard bibs on their chests, unfastened on their backs.

They first warn the relatives softly to disperse. I ask one cop, under whose command (read'on whose leash') these cops are, that how could this sparse, miserable assembly of such people – these timeworn women, fragile old men, innocuous children – endanger the state or law and order. Are they carrying weapons? Have they gathered to dethrone the government with placards and photographs?

Stern-faced, he reacts,'Section 144 – no gathering allowed. Kindly don't lecture. We are on duty. I don't enjoy discussions. Nor am I fond of no's.'

As my colleagues get busy taking notes and pictures, I privately signal Haleema to leave. Everybody follows her.

We meet up at Ahdoos hotel later, the relatives and I. Haleema wants me to be there; an NGO called New Better World wants to be introduced to the relatives. Haleema addresses the team fiercely. Two women and a bald male from the NGO listen to her as if a secret is being divulged to them.

Whenever I see Haleema speaking on behalf of her ilk, she immediately looks more robust, vibrant, vigorous: 'Then they took them…we visited all the jails…camps…but in vain…' The sweat over her brow, the flushed red face, the blood vessels on her throat, the sparkle in her eyes and her invincible spirit – what a woman!

May they deliver, this NGO, to the resolve of her narration! Here in this small valley, NGOs have mushroomed, and some of them – unremarkable, insidious ones – have broken the trust of the people they are supposed to help. They have become number crunchers and alarmists, with their agenda and corporate support. But still…

There is a new face among the relatives, a coughing, middle-aged man who sits furtively behind the gathering of members. I am shocked to learn he is (or was?) Haleema's husband.

It is the hottest day of this summer, or at least it feels like that. Everything smells of the heat. A ruthless midday sun radiates overhead. I drive Haleema to the office of New Better World. She has become a pair of exhausted, languidly rolling eyes in the rear-view mirror.

The NGO's office is lined with tall ornamental cedars in the lawn, pointing towards the heavens like arrows. The gate is closed. There is a big brass lock on the latch, shaped like an eight. A freshly pasted gum-stained notice on the gate cluelessly tells us: New Better World shifted.

Shifted!

I am once again at the Joo house. I knock, once, twice, and nobody answers. My heartbeat picks up and I knock harder and wait. And just a moment before I decide to barge in, I hear a screech of the bolt.

'Sorry, I dozed off,' she says, ushering me inside. 'I want to sleep dreamlessly. I want to rest in peace. Just that. I don't want to know what this world is or whether something like it exists. That is why I sleep as much as I can. I don't want to know about life or death, nor whether I exist or not. I wouldn't want to know what peace is. Just that.'

She has begun talking in a singsong voice. As if everything she says is an endless poem. A free verse.

I am on my way to the Soura hospital.

Haleema has been admitted following complaints of severe chest pain. She has aged suddenly; sunken-eyed, bed-sored, intravaneously fed, she lies on a bed in a corner of the ICU. A diaphanous plastic mask from which a clump of pipes and wires run to a slender oxygen cylinder and a cardiograph has been placed over her mouth and nose.

A thin spiritual-green line zigzags periodically across the black screen of the machine like a Richter scale.

Some women from her group surround her, attending to her. Some are lost in gloom in the corridor outside.

A pink booklet over the foot of the bed reads 'COPD'. I enquire from a visiting doctor about the diagnosis. He explains it as chronic obstructive pulmonary disease. And adds on his own: severe.

When I look back on the 1990s retrospectively, I find the valley enrobed in paradoxes.

Look at the bunkers, meant to disappear one day, now rebuilt in concrete and redbrick for permanence, adorned with potted geraniums and wiremesh windows.

Look at Papa 2, once dreaded torture centre, now a guesthouse for foreign tourists.

People who lived on the banks of the Jehlum have been displaced in the name of development schemes, and the banks renovated to attract tourists.

Everything has changed, except the fate of victims of oppression. Governments have replaced each other. The young have substituted the old. A battalion has taken over from the other.

Yet, a daughter still waits for her father to wed her off. A wife searches for her husband. And a mother still pines for her son and waits for him to be a pallbearer when she dies.

Hope has diminished and uncertainty doubled.

It fills me with rage every day. I feel like making portraits of a seven-year-old battered by the police and hanging them on the walls of the politicians and their galleries. I want to encircle New Delhi with Badami Bagh Cantonment. I want to collect tears of the half mothers and sprinkle them on the faces of Indian journalists. I want to rinse the brains of blinkered Indian elites with the blood of seventy thousand Kashmiris. I want to gift lice-infested blankets from prison cells to the youth in KFCs, McDonalds, Baristas and Café Coffee Days. I want to put up pictures of a flimsy old father tumbling over the stretcher-laden corpse of his dead young son (in a police chase) around two words – Hey Ram – on Raj Ghat.

Alas! I have not internalized!

The last two words Haleema uttered before dying: '*Imran saeba? Aakha?*'

Imran. Have you come?

I remember coming to the Joo house when I had just joined the BBC. It was death I was reporting then, and it is death that I am reporting again. The story of my arriving at, and now departing from – possibly, forever – this place begins and ends with the deaths of two generations.

And the third generation has been missing for more than a decade now.

The house seethes with neighbours and colleagues. Women prepare Haleema for her last journey in a tent in the backyard, giving her the last bath.

Inside, in her melancholic bedroom, her medicine, her fake gold jewellery with its rhinestone baubles and her wire-rimmed glasses rest on the window ledge. Her floral print pheran hangs from a peg behind the door. Her cupboards are locked. Her kitchen is clean.

I pocket her glasses to keep them as souvenir. I have stolen them, but I don't care. If she were alive, she wouldn't have minded.

A tailor sews a shroud from a neat white cotton cloth on the frontyard. A path has emerged where people have trampled on the weeds in the lawn. Hot water boils in large vessels. Some immerse sprigs of a dry aromatic herb in the angrily bubbling water to perfume it. Others take the water to the tarpaulin-veiled tent where an elderly woman carries it inside.

The bier and the Imam arrive together. Cousins and rarely visiting kin arrive too. I imagine Imran visiting the house, hearing of Haleema's death, and sitting quietly in a corner of the verandah, thinking, as if, of a séance with his dead mother. Looking at people placing his mother into the coffin. I shake myself awake only to find my throat choked.

I am the first one to touch the coffin. I lift it up and some young boys from Natipora join me. They seem to know me and speak to me in a respectful tone. 'Say *La illaha ilallaah*,' they tell me.

I hold the pall from the front right corner. The coffin is not that heavy – bones and skin do not make much of a burden. It feels as though we are carrying an empty coffin. For a fraction of a moment I look back and see a grainy gulf of heads following us.

At the Natipora shrine, where the road converges and is wide enough to pack a gathering, we place Haleema parallel to Mecca to recite the *janaaza*. The Imam leads the prayer, sitting across the coffin. Someone sobs and snivels.

After the prayers end, I turn around and scan the people. There he is, Haleema's husband – a quiet and shrivelled creature, trying to remain invisible and unknown. Was it him who cried?

Haleema's grave has been dug beside Ab Jaan's, her father, amid a cluster of irises and their long knife-like leaves. The freshly dug soil makes a mound on the edges of the grave. Some boys open the coffin and gently lower Haleema into her final abode. The undertaker places a soft rock of soil under her head. The last rays of the sun shine on the grave as mourners start tossing handfuls of earth into the rectangular trench.

After the grave has become a fresh knoll of earth, the Imam cockles his beard, as white as snow, with his fingers and raises his hands to recite the *fateha*, prayers for the dead.

Hushed conversations tell her story:

She never celebrated Eid. She said her Eid would be her son's return.

...A very loving lady.

...Very jovial.

...Yet an example of courage.

...Yes, very brave.

...Tragedy over tragedy over tragedy...
Around the grave now, the earth is strewn with clods of soil.
...*Inna lillah'i wa inna ilai'hi raji'un*...
To God we belong and to Him we return...

Acknowledgements

Al-hamdulilah! Thank God! My *salaams*, gratitude and affection go to:

Fareeda and Bashir Ahmad Hafiz, my beloved parents, for believing in me, in this book and for waiting for it.

Urooj Jaan, my loving wife, who suffers whenever I write.

Late Jalaal-ud-Din Hafiz (Bab, who couldn't see this book) and Haji Ghulam Muhammad Dar (Papa, my role model) – my grandfathers, for your belief in me. Never have I come across storytellers like you!

Fahad Shah – for connecting me to Amish.

At Hachette India: Amish Raj Mulmi, the adept editor that you are, for liking it instantly, for efficiently and effectively dealing with the small matters in the entire process of publishing, and for those wonderful lunches. Also, Rohan Chhetri – for proofing the manuscript.

Najm-u-Saher, a wonderful student, for reading the manuscript thrice, for the very useful feedback and for everything you did.

Zahid Rafiq, young friend, neighbour and literary brother, for being the trenchant reader I needed badly.

Sanjay Kak, for devoting time to read the raw draft and for your valuable comments.

Syed Husain Abbas Rizvi, my friend and guide, for shaping my wisdom, for the wonderful times we spent together and for all that ubiquitous *claptrap*.

Shams Imran, friend and colleague, for your support and worthwhile insights, always.

Sheikh Moiza Shafiq, for your attempts to represent the story in art; and Safwat Zargar, Sameer Wani, Wasim Nabi, my amenable students, for volunteering in the end.

Sheikh Irfan Yousuf and Wakas Nazir Khan, my acquiescent, handy ones, for that long, delightful evening.

Warmth and love.